Tease Him

Tease Him

The Man Trap Series
Book Two

BY

OLIVIA JAYMES

www.OliviaJaymes.com

Tease Him

My name is Ashlyn Hill and I'm stuck in an elevator. With an incredibly handsome man. He's nice too. Just the kind of guy that I'm always saying that I wish I could meet.

In any other circumstances I'd flirt and maybe give him my number but not tonight. I'm on an important mission and I need to get to the fifth floor of this building as soon as possible. I have to stop a billionaire geek inventor from demolishing a block of historic homes for one of his metal and glass monstrosities. Cute-elevator guy will have to wait.

My name is Kyle Lewis and I'm the guy in the elevator. My day certainly took a turn for the better when I got stuck with this gorgeous woman. I definitely need to get to know her better. There's just one tiny problem…

I'm the evil guy who wants to mow down all of those old houses. She hates my guts. Winning her over isn't going to be easy, but my parents didn't raise a quitter.

CHAPTER ONE

Ashlyn

MOST OF THE time the university town of Arborville was quiet and peaceful; some might even say boring. Nestled in the corn and cows of the Midwest, the town boasted a major state university and a sweet corn festival every end of summer. It also had a lively and thriving downtown area which is where my business was located.

I wouldn't be bragging to say that I had the funkiest and most successful nostalgia shop in the entire state of Illinois. People all over the country contact me when they need a rare vintage item such as a music album in pristine condition, a pet rock mint in box, or maybe a cool toy from the fifties. If I don't have it, I have the connections that can get it. I'm grateful for the success and I never take it for granted, which was why I was all about giving back to the community.

"It's not going to make any difference," my assistant Katie said with a shake of her head. "They've already made up their minds. They want the jobs the project will bring in, not to mention the prestige of having a technological center right here in Arborville. Kyle Lewis could be the next Elon Musk."

"Kyle Lewis is a pain in my ass and I don't even know the

man. All I know is that he wants to take a wrecking ball to one of the most historic neighborhoods in this town. If I can get the town council to declare that block a historical landmark, he'll have to find another location."

"They're afraid he'll find another *town*."

I shoved a stack of papers into a worn leather messenger bag. I'd been researching this topic for days. I was loaded for bear and ready to make my case.

"There are several other suitable locations," I argued. "In fact, I have three that I can suggest just from my research. And I'm one person. He has a staff of hundreds. He should be able to find a dozen better places for his metal and glass monstrosity."

"You don't know that he's going to build it in metal and glass." Katie tidied up the sales counter. "You're just guessing about that."

"Maybe I'm embellishing a little bit but he's a tech guy. Do you think his new buildings are going to be trimmed in gingerbread? Nope, they're going to be modern and cutting edge or whatever else they call it."

I wasn't the biggest fan of technology. It had its place, of course. I had a computer in the store and great software to keep track of inventory and money. I used the internet a great deal as well and I had a Netflix account. I had a cell phone that my friends forced on me and it was currently at the bottom of my purse. It might even have a charge. I was always forgetting to plug it in.

Technology was not my enemy. But I wasn't stupid and naive enough to think it was my friend, either.

"I just don't want you to be disappointed," Katie said, settling onto the barstool behind the counter and holding out the pink paper. "The council isn't going to change their minds. They're looking at this like it's a feather in the cap of the town."

"I'm completely prepared. I've been working on this for days." I held up the messenger bag. "I have charts, graphs, and reports. I have data. I'm not going to rely on sentiment for this. I have a good case."

"That's good, because Kyle Lewis didn't get where he is by being haphazard and unprepared. He's a genius inventor and supposedly one of the smartest men in the country."

"He also hates anything old," I shot back, slinging the bag over my shoulder. "He's going to take a wrecking ball to those beautiful old homes to make way for something cold and sterile."

Katie sighed and tapped the newspaper. "He certainly doesn't look like a horrible person. Have you seen his picture? He's a hunk and a half."

"I don't have time to moon over a photo. I'll see him in person tonight."

"Speaking of seeing people, did you call your grandmother back?"

I hadn't but I would.

"Not yet. I've been busy with this project."

"She's just going to call back. Is it time for her to visit again? It seems like she was just here."

My grandmother visited twice a year no matter how busy she was. She'd raised me after my mother died and we tried to keep in touch as much as possible despite our crazy schedules.

"She was just here for a few days after Thanksgiving. She's calling to see about the council meeting. She must think it's already happened. I'll call her in the morning." I checked the clock on the wall. "Which is my cue to get out of here. Are you sure you can close up by yourself?"

Laughing, Katie waved away my concerns. "Don't worry about it. I got this covered. We've already put the closed sign on the door and all I need to do it close out the register and lock up. Easy peasy. You're just afraid to delegate."

Katie knew me well. "You're so efficient you're making me obsolete."

"Then take a few days off for a change. You work like a mule and never take any time for yourself. Enjoy the fruits of your labors once in a while."

I kept planning a vacation but somehow, I never actually left.

"I'll think about it. Have a good evening. See you tomorrow."

I slipped out of the back door and walked briskly down the street. City Hall was only three blocks away and to say that the evening was freezing was being polite. January was always cold and gray but the last few days had been especially chilly, the temperature hovering near zero. The cold air seeped up under my skirt, turning my legs blue and making me wish I'd chosen another "professional" outfit. I wanted to impress tonight at the meeting and my usual blue jeans weren't going to do that.

A big gust of wind came up behind me and practically pushed me into the building, a beautiful structure of brick and stone. It had been built just after World War II and it still had the original marble floors. My high heels made loud clicking noises on that floor as I hurried to catch the elevator.

"Hold the elevator, please," I called out, trying not to slip, fall, and make a fool of myself. I didn't wear high heels on a daily basis and I sure didn't make a habit of sprinting in them. Luckily, a hand snaked out of the elevator car at the last minute and pushed the doors open.

It looked like luck was on my side tonight and I wouldn't have to trudge up five flights of stairs.

There was only one other person in the elevator, a tall man with dark blond hair. I couldn't see his face because he was bent over his cell phone. People didn't look each other in the eye anymore. They just stared at their phones. Still, I'd been raised to be polite even if someone else wasn't.

"Thank you. I appreciate you holding the elevator."

"You're welcome. It was cold in the lobby."

The man still didn't look up though, his gaze trained on the piece of technology in his hand while his thumbs tapped out a message that had to be more important than actual human contact.

The elevator was slow at the best of times and it rumbled and shook as it rose. I could hear the familiar whine and grind that the residents of Arborville had come to know and love. This was something that Kyle Lewis would never understand. This building was amazing because of its history. It had a story. Newer buildings simply didn't have the same soul or presence.

The half-circle dial over the doors moved from floor three to four before the elevator car shuddered and came to a halt. I reached over and pushed the number five on the panel again.

And again.

Nothing.

This was not good. I could already feel the walls closing in on me.

"I don't think pushing the button over and over is going to help."

But would it hurt? I was desperate here.

He'd looked up from his phone and I was able to see his face now. Handsome. Warm brown eyes that matched his leather jacket and a nice square jaw covered in well-trimmed scruff. Not quite a beard but definitely not clean shaven. He was dressed casually in blue jeans and a white button-up shirt. Too old to be a student, he appeared to be somewhere in that murky area of his thirties. Maybe a professor?

Either way, he didn't seem to be grasping the seriousness of the situation.

"We're not moving."

His gaze went up to the dial over the doors where the arrow was pointing right above four. So close to my destination it was maddening.

"Because we're stuck."

"Stuck?"

"Stuck." He held up his phone. "I'll call 911. You might want to relax. As old as this elevator is, we could be here for awhile."

Stuck in an elevator. Did I mention my claustrophobia? This was awful. All I needed was a knife-wielding clown to make my nightmare complete.

The nice-looking man dialed and spoke calmly to whomever had answered. My fingers itched to grab the phone from him and plead with the person to get help here quickly but I had to realize that my emergency may not be the worst happening at the moment.

It just *felt* that way.

"They'll be here as soon as they can. They're dispatching the fire department."

An image of me climbing down a ladder while the wind blew my skirt up showing off my lace panties and cellulite ran through my mind, making me cringe.

Note to self: Always dress like you're about to climb a ladder.

I let my heavy messenger bag and purse slide to the floor and took a deep, cleansing breath. These walls weren't going to defeat me. I was fine.

"So I guess we wait. Or maybe we could try and pull the doors apart. I saw that in a movie once."

"And if we're stuck between floors? What then?"

Definitely a professor. Probably in engineering or mathematics. Driven by logic.

"One of us could climb up to the next floor. I mean, if it isn't too far."

He was eyeing the doors as if contemplating my suggestion. "I suppose I could give you a boost."

Another image – of him looking up my skirt this time – crossed my brain. I really needed to stick to pants going forward.

To my shock and surprise, he actually seemed to take me seriously, stepping forward to try and pry the doors apart even shedding his coat beforehand. I couldn't help but admire the play of muscles under his shirt as he tried but sadly failed to pull the doors open. He tried several times, but in the end gave up with a grimace.

"Sorry, they aren't going to budge. Even if I could get these inside doors open there's an outer set as well."

I hadn't seen that part in the movie.

"I appreciate you trying. That was very nice of you."

I was beginning to think he was a very nice man indeed. Nice looking, nice acting. Other than the phone thing, he was well-mannered and I was finding lately that particular trait was becoming as rare as an original, never-opened Led Zeppelin album. I could practically hear my friend Shelby screaming in my ear.

Ask him for coffee.

Show him you're interested.

Shelby was engaged and wanted everyone to be in a happy relationship. She'd even written a how-to manual on how to trap a man. Since I wasn't interested in hunting or trapping anyone, I wasn't her target audience.

I did take a moment, however, to check his left hand for a ring. Nope. He was single.

Single, handsome, and we were stuck in the elevator for who knew how long. Was this the universe smacking me over the head? I was usually oblivious to things like this. Especially when I was stuck in a small confined space that might run out of oxygen. Should I breathe shallowly?

"It's no problem," he assured me with a smile. He had a dimple in his right cheek. Yep, he was cute. Really cute. "I was happy to try. You seem like you're in a big hurry to the fifth floor."

"I am and it's really important that I be there. They're voting on building a tech center here in town. You may have read about it in the newspaper."

I didn't mention the claustrophobia. I didn't want to freak him out thinking that, well...I would freak out. I wasn't going to. I was almost sure of it.

"I think I did read about it. A technology campus, right? Is that a bad thing?"

The newspaper certainly had made it sound like rainbows and unicorns.

"It's a terrible thing. Kyle Lewis wants to tear down several historical homes that have been in Arborville for generations."

Rubbing his chin, he nodded as if he understood. "I don't think you need to worry. They won't vote until Kyle Lewis is there and he's late, too."

"How could you possibly know that?"

His smile widened, full of mirth and mischief. "Because I'm Kyle Lewis."

The universe had a sick sense of humor.

CHAPTER TWO

Kyle

I WAS GOING to straight to hell. Do not pass Go. Do not collect two hundred dollars.

The minute the cute little blonde told me why she was so worried about being late I should have come clean about who I was, but I truly wanted to know what her issue with the tech campus was. I'd seen those old houses when I first came to Arborville scouting locations and it had never occurred to me for a minute that anyone would object to those eyesores being knocked down. They were a safety hazard and, at the very least, they ought to be surrounded by orange cones.

A little like this elevator.

The blonde had dug through her messenger bag and had pulled out a photo of the old homes, holding it up for me as if I'd never seen them for myself.

"These homes need to be saved and restored, not hit with a wrecking ball."

She was cute when she was passionate about something. Her blue eyes sparkled with life and her cheeks were pink. This was important to her so I had to tread lightly, but this was also important to me, too. This tech campus was my dream and locating here in Arborville was a sound decision.

Maybe I could talk to her, help her see how impossible what she wanted was.

"What's your name?"

She gave me a look so suspicious I might as well have been a mugger or a serial killer.

"Ashlyn. Ashlyn Hill."

It was a pretty name but if I said that she'd probably stomp on my foot.

"How long have you lived in Arborville, Ashlyn?"

I liked the way her name slid off my tongue. I'd been giving her what I'd hoped was a covert cursory inspection since the moment she'd stepped into the elevator.

I liked what I saw. Petite, she barely reached my shoulder and I'd caught a glimpse of her legs when she'd reached into her bag and they were killer, but it was her hair that kept drawing my eye. Golden and shiny, I could tell it was long, although at the moment it was pulled into a ponytail away from her delicate features. For four floors I'd been trying to think of something to say that didn't sound corny, stupid, or like a blatant pickup line when the elevator car came to a stuttering halt. This was either my luckiest day or my worst one.

"I moved here to go to the university." Her little chin lifted. Damn, she was cute.

The only problem in this charming little meet-cute was that Ashlyn thought I was scum. An unusual situation to find myself in as since I'd gained a certain amount of fame – and fortune – a couple of years ago when I'd registered a few patents.

"This is a wonderful town," I assured her. "The people are

great. That's why I wanted to locate my tech campus here. I think this would be a terrific place to live."

"It's not exactly New York City."

Thank god. "That's why I chose it."

There was a loud pounding sound on the door and then voices. Rescuers. For a moment, I was annoyed that they'd shown up in such a timely manner. I could have talked to Ashlyn for much longer, but this really wasn't the place to romance a female. As soon as we were out of here, I'd ask her for coffee or dinner. She's turn me down, of course, because she hated me, but I didn't get to where I am because I was a quitter.

"Looks like we're going to get out of here."

Pretty Ashlyn was looking at me like I was something she'd scraped off the bottom of her shoe and she couldn't wait not to share oxygen with me. I was liking her more and more. She had spirit and passion, even if I thought her passion was misguided at the moment.

"It looks like we are," I replied, holding my breath. No matter how successful a guy is with the ladies, he never gets over the fear of asking one out. At least, he shouldn't. I sure as hell never have, especially when I'm aware of the likely outcome. "I don't suppose you'd want to grab a coffee when we get out of here?"

"I don't think that's a good idea but thank you."

Polite but firm. I wouldn't push but...

"You can tell me all about why I shouldn't locate my tech campus where those houses are."

For a second she looked tempted but then shook her head.

"I don't think that's a genuine offer."

"It is but I understand your reticence." I pulled a business card out of my pocket and handed it to her. "If you change your mind, give me a call. I'm always interested in listening to good ideas and contrary to your opinion of me, Ashlyn, I do have an open mind."

She didn't get a chance to respond. The doors on the elevator slid open, showing that we were indeed stuck between floors. Three firefighters were peering into the elevator car.

"You folks okay?" asked the one in the middle. "We got the doors open as quickly as we could."

"We're fine," I assured him, glancing at Ashlyn who appeared to be relieved. "But I think we're ready to get out of here."

We both had a meeting to attend.

"Ladies first," the firefighter said, beckoning to Ashlyn. "We'll have you out of here in no time."

He was true to his word. Within ten minutes we were both out and standing on the fifth floor. The meeting was already in progress, the double doors closed. My friend George was sure to be in there, hopefully charming the town council until I arrived. I'd shot him a text from the elevator telling him to stall. If anyone could do it, he could.

We thanked the firefighters and they left, but not before stringing some yellow tape in front of the elevator doors. Everyone would be taking the stairs tonight.

"So I guess this is it," I said to Ashlyn, who was smoothing down her skirt. She looked nervous and I had to admit that I wasn't feeling super comfortable myself. I'd hoped this vote might go smoothly but she might only be the tip of the iceberg. Were there hundreds of people that didn't want me or my business in Arborville? I might leave this meeting disappointed.

"I guess it is."

"Well, good luck."

"You too."

I opened one of the double doors and stepped aside. "After you, Ashlyn Hill."

"Thank you."

Ashlyn entered the conference room and I followed right behind, relieved to see George sitting right up front and smiling. Things couldn't be too bad if he was happy. In fact, the entire town council was smiling, some even grinning at my entrance. I could feel it in my gut.

This vote was going my way.

And Ashlyn Hill was going to hate me even more before this night was over.

★ ★ ★

Ashlyn

I DUG MY fork into the pile of pulled barbecue brisket and then shoved a huge bite into my mouth. I was upset and angry. Food was my only comfort at the moment.

I'd lost.

Not officially. The final vote would be held next month but the preliminary vote had been almost unanimous. The one hold out voter was Old Man Hendrick who I swear was ancient when I was a child and heaven only knew his age now. He voted no on pretty much everything because he was cantankerous that way. The preliminary vote cleared the way for Kyle Lewis to start getting architectural drawings and bids.

I was having a huge plate of barbecue after the meeting with my two best friends, Shelby Kelly and Emerson Grant. They'd been waiting for me outside the meeting and immediately upon seeing my defeated expression had spirited me away to the barbecue dive we often frequented for a much-needed junk food infusion.

I assumed Kyle Lewis would be celebrating his victory with fine champagne and lobster.

Shelby and Emmy hadn't said too much, letting me stuff my face until I was ready to talk.

I was ready.

"It's not fair. The council didn't even want to hear from me. All they care about is jobs, jobs, jobs."

Shelby nodded sympathetically. "That's how they get elected, hon. No one is going to vote for them because they saved an old rundown neighborhood on the edge of town."

"It's historic."

Emmy patted my hand. "Not everything that's old is historic. Sometimes it's just...old. If you had all the money in the world you might be able to save them but otherwise they're just rotting away and pulling down house values."

I looked up from my brisket and glared at my friend. Whose side was she on, anyway?

"If George Washington slept in one of those houses they wouldn't tear them down."

"But he didn't," Emmy replied. "And even if he had I'm sure George Washington slept a whole bunch of places in his life that they've paved over now."

"With friends like you…"

"We are your friends," Shelby argued. "But you need to see that you're wasting your time and energy on this fight, Ash. People want and need jobs. The council would be derelict in its duties if it didn't allow this project to move forward. You need to pick a battle that you can actually win."

I stabbed another piece of meat with my fork. "He looked so smug, too. He knew he'd won and he was smiling. Arrogant asshole."

Emmy and Shelby exchanged a glance before the former piped up. "Who's an asshole?"

"Kyle Lewis. Smug jerk." Although he'd actually been really nice in the elevator. "Do you know he asked me for coffee? Can you believe that he had the nerve to do that?"

Eyes wide, Emmy took a gulp of her iced tea. "Wait a cotton-picking minute. You said you were stuck in the elevator with him. We assumed it was for a few minutes. Just how long were in there with him? And you turned him down?"

"Of course, I turned him down. He's the enemy. My nemesis."

"He's almost handsome, rich, and a freaking genius," Shelby pointed out. "If I wasn't engaged I'd have coffee with him."

"You don't know him like I do."

Emmy cleared her throat. "I think you need to start at the beginning and tell us all the details. You've skipped over some major parts of the story. Important facts that we need to know. Why don't you start when you entered the elevator?"

That's where it all went downhill.

CHAPTER THREE

Kyle

'D WON AND I was happy as hell about it. The final vote hadn't been taken yet but there didn't appear to be any hurdles in my way to making my dream a reality. Arborville was my new home and I couldn't wait to get started.

George and I had decided to get a bite after the meeting. I'd been too busy earlier to eat and now my stomach was growling and letting me know that I'd better feed it right the hell now. Of course, there was only one place we wanted to go – the hole in the wall barbecue joint we'd accidentally found months ago when we'd first visited Arborville. We'd both been starving, and we'd stumbled on the jewel as we'd toured the downtown area. I didn't know who was manning their kitchen but whomever it was knew their way around a smoker. The brisket was positively melt in your mouth.

The walk to the restaurant, however, was freezing cold. My cheeks were red from the wind and by the time we pushed open the door and felt the rush of warm air greet us we were chilled to the bone. Midwest cold felt distinctly different than a New York City cold. It had to be that prairie wind that got deep inside and didn't let go without a fight.

The hostess showed us to our table and the waitress quickly and efficiently took our order. We were both having the brisket, although I was contemplating getting a rack of ribs to take home and nibble on the next day. Or maybe even tonight. I didn't sleep much, my mind always whirling and gnawing on problems. Thankfully, I didn't need much sleep or maybe I'd learned to live without it. Either way, those ribs might not make it 'till dawn.

George's brows were raised and his head jerked slightly to the left. "Isn't that her?"

I followed his gaze to where my elevator buddy Ashlyn Hill was sitting with two other females. She didn't look nearly as happy as I did, and I suddenly felt a little guilty for my euphoria. My win was her loss, but she shouldn't be discouraged. She'd fought admirably and had made some decent points.

I was actually going to have someone go in and take another look at those houses to see if they were as bad as they looked or if they were salvageable. I just wasn't planning on telling her about it. I didn't want to raise her hopes because I had a pretty good idea what I was going to find out.

I was sure those homes were not only rundown, they were dangerous. Frankly, I'd be doing the city a favor tearing them down. One stray spark and the whole block would go up like a box of tinder.

"Yes," I said, my gaze settling on the three women. "That's Ashlyn Hill."

George was grinning comically. "She doesn't like you."

"I'm so glad you're finding this hilarious."

"I don't remember the last female that didn't like you. This is positively historic. Dear Diary, there's a female in this world that didn't fall for Kyle's fame and fortune today. She's immune to his charm. She thinks he's evil."

Evil might be taking it too far, but she didn't like me, that's for sure.

"I can't even argue with you. She turned me down like a bad habit. Talk about an ego buster."

"You have plenty of self-esteem. You'll survive. So what are you going to do now?"

Good question. The never-say-die part of me wanted to keep trying, wear her down with my charm. Another part of me overrode that one however, saying that behavior wasn't respectful. She'd said no. End of story.

I did find her fascinating, though. Not many people would have shown up at that meeting to take me on. Ashlyn Hill had been all by herself, too. No environmental organizations backing her, no anti-tech groups with picket signs extolling the virtues of analog-anything. Just her and me, toe to toe.

That wasn't really accurate. The town council had been firmly on my side. Jobs and all. They'd politely let her speak but I don't think most of them were really listening except for that one old guy at the end of the row who had voted no. I had the distinct impression that he didn't like me, either.

"I'm not going to do anything. She turned me down and thinks I'm lower than a snake's belly. It's hard to come back from that, my friend. Best thing I can do is accept defeat gracefully." I playfully wagged my finger at him. "No one likes a sore loser."

George glanced over at the table with the three women, as

did I. Ashlyn looked much happier and I was glad her friends could cheer her up.

"She is pretty."

She was. She was intelligent, too. I could tell from her presentation. Her sense of humor was still questionable but I had a feeling that it was fine from the way she was smiling at something one of her friends said.

"Lots of women are pretty, George. Plenty of fish in the sea."

"I don't think you're as okay with this as you pretend to be," George chuckled. "I think this bugs you."

"A man shouldn't have everything he wants," I replied, quoting my father. He was always warning me about getting spoiled because of my success. "It's not healthy. Caesar had everything he wanted and look what happened to him."

"A cautionary tale," George agreed. "Now how about we talk about the campus? I've had another idea that I think you might like."

This was good. Back to business. No more thinking about delicate blondes with stubborn chins that thought pressing an elevator button over and over again was going to make the car move.

She simply wasn't interested.

★ ★ ★

Ashlyn

THAT STUPID MAN trap book.

Shelby was currently extolling its virtues, reminding us that her sister Mia had used it and was now blissfully living in

Scotland with the man of her dreams. Shelby had a Ph.D. and was a licensed clinical therapist, which usually meant that she would try and figure out our hidden motivations. For example, I couldn't have eaten because I was hungry. I must have been trying to swallow my anger along with a large pizza with extra cheese.

At some point in the past after a few margaritas, Emmy and I had agreed to help Shelby when she finished her book. I think I can speak for my friend when I say that we never thought Shelby would finish the book, so when she did we were trapped. Mia had been the first to succumb and admittedly it had worked out for her. She was in love and planning a life with her man and we were all ecstatic for her. But that didn't mean that it would work for me.

"And I also don't have to remind you that you both promised to help me vet the book when it was finished," Shelby said. "The book is done, it worked for Mia, now it's time to step up and do your part. One person working through the book isn't enough. Three isn't really enough but at least it's a start."

My word meant something to me, so I was basically backed into a corner. I simply couldn't let Shelby down.

"I'll take a look at it," I said with a heavy put-upon sigh. Just a little dramatic. "But I can't promise that I'll use anything. Besides, I'm not even dating anyone right now."

"That's your own fault," Emmy said. "You could be out with Kyle Lewis right this very minute."

"I doubt we have much in common," I replied with an eye roll. "He's probably sipping champagne and dining on lobster in celebration."

"I think he's more of a barbecue brisket kind of guy," Emmy said with a grin. "Ask me how I know."

"Okay, how do you know?"

Emmy nodded toward my left. "Because he and some other guy are sitting at the table right over there."

The universe was clearly messing with me and I was starting to get peeved. Out of all the restaurants in Arborville he had to walk into this one. Shelby's lips pursed and her eyes widened as her gaze ran over my nemesis. He seemed to notice my regard and raised his hand in a wave that almost had me scurrying under the table to hide. There he was, smiling and waving like we were buddies. We were not. I quickly turned away and hid my face behind a menu card.

"Wow, that is one handsome man. And he's a genius?"

Emmy nodded. "Rich and successful, too. He's the whole package."

Shelby's gaze had now settled on me. "And you turned him down? Have you lost your mind?"

They didn't get it, which surprised me. They usually totally understood my little quirks but this time they were letting the tasty candy coating blind them to what lay underneath.

"Can you imagine the two of us on a date?" They hadn't thought this through. "What would we talk about? We don't have anything in common. He's not my type."

Emmy's brows shot up. "Honey, he's everyone's type, and you don't have to marry him. Just go for coffee. There's no commitment there."

I snuck another glance at Kyle Lewis from the corner of my eye. He was extremely good-looking and I'd been interested until

I found out who he really was. But that was the key phrase… *who he really was.* He was a man that only looked forward, not appreciating the past.

"We don't have anything in common," I repeated, more firmly this time. "It would be a disaster. We'd end up arguing and hating each other. He's my nemesis, the enemy, for heaven's sake."

"He obviously has an open mind," Emmy said. "He asked you for coffee knowing full well that you would probably use that time to try and convince him that he was wrong and you were right. Maybe you should take advantage of that."

"Are you suggesting that I use my womanly wiles to change his mind about the location for the tech campus?"

Shelby's gaze wandered back to where the two men were seated. They were both smiling and laughing over their brisket. Of course, Kyle Lewis had good reason to be happy. He'd won tonight. The battle, not the war.

"I think Emmy is just saying that if he's offered you his time, you should take it. You never know. You might find that you actually like him and enjoy the date."

I swear sometimes talking to my friends was like talking to a wall.

"Name me one thing that Kyle Lewis and I have in common. Just one."

Emmy waved her fork toward the two men. "Well, you both ordered the exact same dinner. That's a start."

"It's not a start," I denied, although I had to admit he had decent taste in food. But on what planet did that constitute a reason to date someone? "There is no start here. I am not going out with him. Ever."

Shelby pulled the black binder from her incredibly oversized handbag and slapped it on the table between them. "Take it just in case. You never know when you might need it."

"A dating emergency?" I asked. If I rolled my eyes again they were going to get stuck and I wasn't sure if my health insurance would cover it. "How many of those happen on a regular basis?"

Shelby nodded over to Kyle Lewis, who was now charming the waitress just like he had the town council. "He might ask you out again."

"And I'll say no again. I'm not interested. If you like him so much, you date him."

The less I saw of Kyle Lewis the better.

CHAPTER FOUR

Kyle

"HAVE YOU LISTENED to a word I've said?"

With a sigh, I had to admit the answer was a resounding no. I hadn't heard a word that George had said, my mind on other subjects.

Well…one in particular. Ashlyn Hill. I couldn't stop thinking about her. She really and truly hated my guts. It gave me a chuckle when I remembered how she'd hid behind that menu at the barbecue place when I'd had the audacity to wave at her.

"I'm a little distracted right now. Maybe we could talk about this later."

George reached for the coffee pot on my kitchen island. New to town, I still didn't have an office space so I was working out of my new home.

"You don't even know what *this* is. I could be telling you that I've decided to get rid of all of my worldly goods and join a monastery for all you know."

An image of George with a shaved head drifted through my mind. It wasn't a good look for the guy.

"Are you? Because if you do, I want your drum set."

"I like wine, women, and song way too much do ever do

that. But if I did, my drum set is going with me, asshole."

George did love his parties, but I wasn't sure how well the monks were going to like him whaling on his drums whenever he was stuck on a problem. Of course, he wouldn't have any problems if he joined a monastery.

"Nice attitude for a monk. Seriously, what were we talking about?"

"*We* weren't talking about anything. I was talking and you were daydreaming. The last time that happened you invented a rocket that didn't need rocket fuel, so you have me intrigued."

"I didn't actually invent it. I have some preliminary schematics. It needs more work. Lots more."

At the rate I was going, my grandchildren might figure out the issues.

"So what were you thinking about?"

I shrugged, pacing around the kitchen. I wasn't in the mood to sit down and deal with the business side of Lewis Technology, Inc. Maybe I'd grab my sweats and running shoes and go work off some energy.

"Everything. There's a lot going on if you haven't noticed."

Since the town council had voted in my favor three days ago it had been a whirlwind of activity, mostly garnering bids from architects. I wanted to break ground in the spring and I'd already been told – by several people – that the timeline was insane.

Okay, they'd said unreasonable but wasn't that the same thing? That was the problem with society today. No one wanted to make the impossible possible. No one wanted to see what they could do if they put their mind to it. Everyone wanted to take the safe route.

The road constantly traveled and well-known.

"I had noticed." My friend was giving me a strange look, his eyes narrow as if he were studying me which was ridiculous because other than my family, George knew me better than anyone. "You were thinking about that woman again."

It wasn't phrased as a question. But as I just said, George knew me well.

"A little," I admitted. I wasn't quite ready to cop to exactly how much I'd been thinking about her these last few days. There was just something about her that intrigued me. It wasn't her looks, although she was beautiful. Beautiful women were everywhere. It was the strength and determination I'd seen inside of her as she'd stood up in front of that town council and presented her case. She'd known the odds were against her and she'd done it anyway, fully believing in her cause. And she'd done a damn good job, too. Hell, she'd almost convinced me. Almost. "She made a compelling argument. Did you have a team go look at that block of houses?"

"I did and am waiting on the report." George stood from his seat at the island and walked over to where he'd tossed his briefcase on the couch, pulling out a sticky note. "I had a feeling you wouldn't be able to put Ms. Ashlyn Hill out of your head. You don't like to lose. It bugs the shit out of you."

"That's not why I'm thinking about her."

Was it? I didn't want to think that I was so shallow that I couldn't take getting turned down for a date.

"Fine, that's not why." He slapped the sticky note on the marble island. "If you're interested, that's her place of business. She owns a retro shop in the downtown area, and damn successful, too. She has the largest inventory of vinyl records in the Midwest. You could also pick up a pet rock. I know you've been talking about getting a pet now that you're settled into your new home and have a yard."

"I was thinking about a dog, not a rock."

He wagged his finger at me. "This is your problem. You're too picky."

"That is not my problem."

"It is," he declared, wearing a shit-eating grin. He was loving this. "You're never satisfied. A pet rock would require none of your time or effort. Think of the advantages."

"I am not going to Ashlyn Hill's store to buy a pet rock." He reached for the sticky note but I beat him to it, peeling it from the marble and holding it up. "But I would like to add to my collection of records. How about we go out and get a bite to eat and then swing by the store?"

Purely for research.

★ ★ ★

I SHOULD HAVE been doing the monthly paperwork for the store. There was always way too much to do and today was no exception. I had a small office set up in the back room, although I did most of it in my home office. I couldn't seem to resist the allure of the sales floor, talking to customers and straightening the shelves. This was my store and I'd built it over the years. I was proud of it and I admit that I liked showing it off a little when people stopped in. Located in a university town, there was a fresh crop of newcomers every fall.

But I wasn't doing my paperwork. I was sitting behind the counter with Katie reading Shelby's manual on how to trap a man. Just as Mia had said, the beginning was more than a trifle old-fashioned. Not that I minded that. I'd always considered myself an old-fashioned type female. I really wasn't the type to call a man or ask him out on a date. I also liked it when a man held the door for me or brought flowers. I believed in equality, but I liked the romantic touches. I was fully ready to return the favor with a nice shoulder massage or a good meal.

Katie peered over my shoulder as I turned the page to a new chapter. "There's some good advice in this book. That one about not settling for less is pure gold."

Mia would agree. It had been that particular passage in the book that had revolutionized her relationship with Josh and the entire world in general. She didn't accept anything less than the best from him and wonder of wonders…she got it.

"Does Leo put effort into your relationship?"

Leo and Katie had been dating about six months and at first, he was all she could talk about. Lately, not so much.

"He did at the beginning but then it seemed like he started to get too comfortable. Like he'd caught me and that meant he didn't have to do anything afterward. He never wanted to go out. He only wanted to stay home and watch Netflix, eating whatever I had cooked. In the end, he was too cheap to even spring for takeout. I kicked him to the curb a few weeks ago."

Now I felt terrible bringing him up. "I had no idea. I'm so sorry I even said his name."

The pretty brunette didn't look especially heartbroken,

though. "It happens. I'm just glad that I realized he wasn't the one before I got in too deep."

"You two had so much in common. It's a shame it didn't work out. But onward and upward, right?"

"Right," Katie agreed. "What about you? Who are you going to try these ninja dating moves on? How about the UPS man? He's cute."

"Married. Three kids."

"Really? I'll scratch him off the list. Wait...how about that guy that keeps coming in here to see you? The one that wears the Blue Oyster Cult t-shirts."

I knew who she was referring to and she had to be out of her mind. Him? No. Never.

"I can tell you've never spoken to him. He lives with his mother."

"Ouch," Katie winced. "He's off the list as well."

"Before you go too far, there is no one on the list. I'm only reading this book because I promised Shelby I would. She's been driving me and Emmy crazy, especially since Mia left for Scotland a few weeks ago."

"So you're not looking for a man."

"Decidedly not. I have a very busy life. Now if one wants to come find me, that's completely different. I don't think the odds are in my favor, however."

"You mean if Mr. Right just walked through the door?" Katie laughed. "Wouldn't that be great? No bars or online apps. Just a terrific guy delivered directly to your front door. You know, this might be a great idea for a business."

Sometimes Katie could be so innocent and naive but I absolutely adored her.

"It's already been done and it's also highly illegal."

At first, she looked confused and then her eyes widened as understanding dawned. "I didn't mean it like that. I was just thinking about a really cool dating service."

"I bet that's what they tell the judge."

The bell over the door dinged, interrupting our conversation. I turned to smile and greet our customer but almost choked on my spit instead. This couldn't be happening. I'd obviously pissed someone off, perhaps cutting them off in traffic, and they'd placed a curse on me. It was the only explanation for the last few days of my life. Did I need to sacrifice a chicken? I could pick up a bucket on my way home with a side of mashed potatoes and gravy.

"Hello, Ashlyn. We meet again."

It was Kyle Lewis – my nemesis. Thanos to my Captain America. Joker to my Batman. Eddie Haskell to my Beaver.

Oh wait… I didn't mean it like that.

He was standing there with a big smile on his face as if everything in the world was rainbows and kitten whiskers. I was sure he hadn't wandered in to my store by accident. He had to be up to something.

What on earth did he want?

CHAPTER FIVE

Kyle

I WASN'T SURE what I was expecting from Ashlyn Hill's store but this...this wasn't it.

It was utterly fantastic and I had to pick my jaw up from the floor. The entire twentieth century encapsulated in one building. I could have browsed in there for hours and never become bored. Organized by decade, the large space had anything and everything a retro lover could ever want and several things I hadn't ever heard of. There were old calendars, copper pots and pans, glassware, flatware, dishes, furniture, magazines such as *Life* or *Ladies' Home Journal*, old books, novelty items, toys, vintage clothing, and yes, there were even a few Pet Rocks.

But that wasn't the most amazing part of the store. That distinction easily belonged to the large wall at the back which was filled floor to ceiling with racks of vinyl albums, some used and some brand new, still in the original packaging. I could happily spend the rest of my day rummaging through these shelves and I just might do that, work be damned.

"Impressive," George murmured. He had to be as blown away as I was. "This is...something else."

Ashlyn Hill stepped forward, her features calm but I could

tell she was disturbed by my appearance.

"Welcome to Past Perfect. Can I help you find something today?"

Although she'd shown herself to be completely immune to my charm that didn't stop me from trying it again. I smiled and tried to make myself seem as friendly as possible, not like the house-mowing-down-jerk that she seemed to think I was.

"This is amazing, absolutely amazing." My fingers ran over the handlebars of a restored red, white and blue Schwinn bicycle with a banana seat and a basket in the front. I remembered seeing a picture of one of my older cousins riding a bike just like that, only it was green.

"Are you interested in the bicycle, Mr. Lewis? It's an original from 1976 with a Bicentennial motif. I've been assured there are less than a dozen of these left in the United States."

I believed it. I'd never seen anything like it. I wanted to buy it just to display it in my home.

"My mom and dad told me all about how crazy America went for the bicentennial celebration. Everything was red, white, and blue," I replied, dragging my gaze from the bike to Ashlyn. She looked lovely today, even better than the other night. She was dressed far more casually in blue jeans and a soft pink sweater, her long blonde hair swept up in some sort of messy bun. Strands had escaped its confines and had fallen around her cheeks and I had the strangest urge to reach out and smooth them back. I didn't do it, though. She'd probably take my arm off like a tiger. "And my name is Kyle. Mr. Lewis is my dad, and my grandpa."

"If you're looking for bicentennial items we have an entire

section devoted to that." I couldn't seem to drag my gaze from her full lips that were shiny from gloss. It matched her fuzzy sweater. "Mr. Lewis?"

This was becoming a habit – checking out while people were talking to me. Normally I was more alert and focused than any ten human beings ought to be but this woman had me acting out of character. And I barely knew her.

"Kyle," I said again, giving myself an internal smack on the head. Time to straighten up. She hated my guts so there was no point in mooning over her like she was the head cheerleader and I was the president of the chess club. And I *had* been the president of the chess club in high school. "I think I'd like to check out your vinyl collection."

"Of course, follow me. Is there any particular type of music you're interested in?"

I was avidly interested in the gentle sway of her hips as she led us to the back of the store. Her pert little bottom had my full attention, encased in that snug denim. I was reminded again just how petite Ashlyn Hill really was. I had a foot of height on her at the very least.

I'm a complete and total perv. Climb out of the gutter, Kyle.

George elbowing me in the ribs let me know that I hadn't answered her question. I was a mess. Clearly, I had been too long between women. I made a mental note to call one of the ladies in my contacts list and set up a date.

"Classic rock."

There were hundreds of albums and forty-fives. Ashlyn slipped away, leaving me and George in vinyl heaven. I was no hipster, but this was one item from the past that I enjoyed. My dad had a huge album collection and I'd grown up listening to it almost every day of my young life. Dad had never moved on to cassettes, CDs, or digital music. He wasn't stubborn about it but when I'd suggested that I might buy him an iPod one year for Christmas he'd simply shook his head no.

Some things, son, don't need to be improved. They're fine just the way they are. Wisdom is knowing which is which.

Those words had stuck with me through the years and I'd hoped that I'd taken them to heart.

Ashlyn had disappeared back behind the counter, looking busy with a stack of papers, but every now and then I could feel her gaze resting on my back when she was sure I wasn't looking. She might not like me much but I had her attention.

Or maybe she was afraid that I'd shoplift.

An hour later, both George and I each had a stack of albums, plus he had also picked out a Motley Crue tour t-shirt circa 1989.

"We need to come here every weekend," George said, grinning from ear to ear. He placed his items on the counter next to mine. Ashlyn had disappeared and we were being waited on by a pretty girl named Katie, if her name tag was to be believed. "My parents would love that jukebox in their basement. I never know what to get them for Christmas."

That was true. Last year after much debate and two trips to the mall, George had given them a cashier's check. Luckily his parents didn't seem to mind their son's quirky ways and used the money for a vacation to Hawaii.

A door was open behind Katie and I could see back into a storeroom with boxes stacked everywhere. Ashlyn was holding a clipboard and checking off items on a shelf. I can only put it down to temporary insanity, but I abandoned my albums and slipped past Katie and through that door. I had an unrelenting urge to speak to Ashlyn even as a little voice whispered in my ear, *This isn't going to go well.*

"Hey."

Wow. I was so smooth with the ladies. I felt like I was in high school all over again. I'd thought I'd moved past the awkward stage but apparently not.

Clutching that clipboard against her chest as if for dear life, Ashlyn sighed and turned to face me. Yep, I really wasn't this female's favorite person. I wouldn't go so far as to say she loathed me but...

What I was about to do was incredibly stupid. As in really dumb. I just couldn't help myself.

"Hello. Did you need anything?"

There was a whole list of things I needed but I doubt that's what she was referring to. I decided to ignore the question.

"Your store is fantastic. Really amazing. Both George and I could spend the day here."

As stupid as I was about the human condition, I wasn't totally brainless. People like compliments and Ashlyn was no exception. Her cheeks turned a becoming shade of pink and her grip on the clipboard lessened slightly.

"Thank you. We appreciate our customers."

She sounded like a brochure, not the woman who had spoken so passionately at the town council meeting just a few days before. She was nervous and frankly so was I. There was sweat pooling on the back of my neck and I had to resist the urge to sniff my armpits. Had my deodorant given up the ghost at some point this morning? I couldn't remember the last time I was this nervous around the female species.

But I here I was trying to gather the courage to ask her out. Again.

Nervously clearing my throat, I moved closer and caught a whiff of her perfume. It wasn't at all as I would have expected it to be. If asked, I would have said it would be light and floral but it wasn't that at all. It was soft but sensual, exotic and musky. It spoke of hidden mysteries and even deeper desires. If I hadn't been under this woman's spell before I would have been now.

"I'm sorry we got off to such a rocky start," I said, rubbing my sweaty palms against the denim of my jeans. "We should get to know one another better."

Her eyes narrowed with suspicion. "Why?"

Yeah, why? I really didn't think this through.

"Because we seemed to get along in the elevator before you knew who I was."

Her gaze skittered away before returning. "I think you know why."

"I know that you don't support what I'm doing but there's more to me than just this project, Ashlyn. I think there's more to you, too."

"You want me to just forget what you're doing?"

"No, but we can talk about it. I can tell you why certain decisions were made and you can tell me why I'm wrong."

Ashlyn was tempted. I could tell. For just a moment she appeared to want to say yes but then she shook her head and clutched that clipboard more protectively against her chest.

"I don't think it's a good idea."

Anyone else would have stuck his tail between his legs and slunk away. Not me. I was a glutton for punishment when it came to this female.

"Just coffee," I suggested. "Not a full meal. Just a cup of coffee and maybe a pastry. You can talk the entire time and convince me that I'm making a mistake."

Her head tilted to the side as if contemplating the veracity of my offer. "If I was right would you even admit it?"

"Absolutely."

"But you don't think that I am right?"

Well…no.

"I've had experts study this project and I think we're doing the right thing. But I am open to your argument against it."

Slapping the clipboard down on a shelf, Ashlyn pulled herself up to her full height, which was still tiny.

"I don't need to be coddled or mollified. You've heard my arguments against your project and they failed to sway you in any way, so I think coffee, lunch, tea, dinner, or any other form of food and beverage would be a waste of time. I do, however, appreciate your patronage of Past Perfect and you're welcome to shop here anytime during regular business hours. We don't accept personal checks. Now if you'll excuse me I have work to do."

With that, she turned on her heel and marched to the back of the storeroom and out of sight behind towering stacks of boxes. I stood there for a moment digesting the mammoth smackdown I'd just received before also turning and heading back into the store where George and my albums were waiting for me.

Ashlyn Hill wasn't interested. Full stop. The sooner I wrapped my mind around that fact the better off I'd be. Time to move on. There were too many fish in the sea to worry about one pretty blonde.

With pink cheeks. And pillowy lips. And a feisty intelligent nature.

Shit. This was bad. So very bad. Now what?

CHAPTER SIX

Ashlyn

I SHOVED A handful of popcorn into my mouth as we found our seats in the theatre. Emmy, Shelby, and I had decided to see the latest chick flick and after the day I'd had at the shop I needed the distraction.

"What did he expect me to say?" I asked, fiddling with the controller on my seat. "There was no way I was going to say yes to coffee or anything else."

Shelby stole some of my popcorn. She always said she didn't want it and then ended up eating ours.

"Why? He seems like a decent enough guy. He's smart, successful, and he has his own teeth and hair. At least, it looks like he does. Men like him don't grow on trees, you know. Do you have a better offer?"

No, but... I couldn't go out on a date, even a casual coffee date, with my mortal enemy.

"We don't have anything in common."

There were two older couples sitting in the row in front of us and they seemed inordinately interested in our conversation. One of the women wasn't even trying to hide it, having twisted around in her seat to look back at us.

"How do you know?" Emmy asked. "You've barely talked to him and only about one subject. You might have lots in common."

"I doubt it."

The woman in front of us didn't appear to agree. She desperately wanted to say something, but her husband elbowed her and whispered something in her ear causing her to turn to the front again. But she was still listening.

"You're being stubborn," Shelby scoffed. "I'm sure there's more to Kyle Lewis than what you've read about in magazines and newspapers. He's an actual human being and I bet there are many things that he likes that you do, too."

The mention of Kyle Lewis had the woman's head whipping around again, her jaw slack with shock. What? Was it so hard to believe that he might ask me out? Was I that ugly?

Emmy cleared her throat and gave the woman a look that would have had me cowering in the bathrooms. Her cheeks red, she turned back...again. But she was still listening.

"Like what? Ice cream? Everyone likes ice cream."

"I like cake better," Emmy said with a laugh. "Too much dairy for me. But seriously, you should go. He said that he'd listen to your arguments. Why would you pass up that chance?"

Another good question that I'd been asking myself since this morning. Mostly I didn't think it would do any good but there was a part of me that held onto hope that it might.

"He won't change his mind," I finally answered. "It's just a ruse to get me to go out with him."

Shelby's mouth fell open in mock horror. "What a terrible person he must be. Asking you out and offering to let you do all the talking. He's some kind of monster, I tell you. Run far and fast."

This time the woman and her friend had turned around fully in their seats and were gaping at us. Their poor husbands looked like they wanted to dig a hole and jump in. Emmy wasn't one to mess around, though. Smiling sweetly, she held out her box of opened candy to the ladies.

"Sno-Cap?"

These poor women were going to have whiplash by the time the previews ran. I distinctly heard one of the men whisper, "Mind your own business."

Good advice. Too bad Shelby and Emmy weren't going to take it. They had a bee in their bonnet about me and Kyle Lewis.

"He's not a monster," I conceded. "I just can't imagine that we would have a good time. I don't want to go out with someone and argue the whole time."

Shelby was already shaking her head. "Why would you argue the entire time? I'm sure you could find some common ground. I don't agree with Brad about every little thing, but I can still be with him. For example, I'm not fond of his political views and I can't fathom how he doesn't like sweets, but we don't argue about it. When we first dated, we talked about other things. We simply learned about each other. You can like people that you disagree with. Can you imagine only surrounding yourself with people just like you? How boring. You don't want to become one of those people that only want to be around others that agree with them. That's an echo chamber and as a mental health professional I can't recommend it."

I didn't want to think that I was the type of person that

needed everyone to agree with them. I'd always enjoyed a healthy debate of ideas with my friends, but Kyle Lewis wasn't my friend.

"It doesn't matter. He's not going to ask me out again."

Not after the way I'd turned him down. I hadn't meant to be so nasty and cold, but he'd thrown me by inviting me out again and I hadn't known how to deal with it. I wasn't great in crunch mode. I was a planner by nature and when I had to act off the cuff, it didn't always work out well.

"He probably won't," Emmy agreed as the theater lights dimmed. A hotdog and a soda started dancing on the screen and the two couples in front of us appeared to be more interested in them than us. "I doubt he enjoys getting turned down. I bet it doesn't happen often. I doubt you'll see him again unless he wants to buy more records."

That was fine with me. Better than fine. I was thrilled that I wouldn't be dealing with Kyle Lewis again.

So how come I felt so let down?

★ ★ ★

A GIANT BOUQUET of beautiful, fragrant flowers in a lovely crystal vase.

That's what was sitting on my kitchen table after a harried delivery man had dropped them off this morning. I was sure this was some sort of mistake, but it was my name clearly on the envelope. The darn thing weighed a ton and I'd hefted it onto the table and opened the card.

They were from Kyle Lewis.

Honest to frog, I never would have guessed that these were from him, especially after I'd delivered that dick punch when he'd asked me out yesterday. If anything, I should have expected a horse head in my sheets.

The sentiment on the card was simple and straightforward written in a bold hand.

Please reconsider my invitation. I'd very much like to discuss the project with you or any other subject you might care to talk about. Kyle

The flowers really were gorgeous, and I hated myself for loving them. He hadn't sent anything so conventional as roses. Roses were fine, but they weren't my favorite flower. Instead he'd chosen brightly-colored, jewel-toned blooms I didn't even recognize but had the most heady and exotic scent. I couldn't seem to stop myself from taking a deep whiff every time I passed by the arrangement.

However, I was no pushover for a few posies. He was still taking a wrecking ball to bunch of historic homes so that made him a jerk, no matter how good his taste in floral decor.

I also wasn't going to admit that he might be the reason that I hadn't slept so well last night. I'd tossed and turned until the wee hours of the morning and it didn't have anything to do with him. I simply couldn't get the room the right temperature and I might need a new mattress and pillow. Plus, I had a great deal on my mind and long to-do list now that the holidays were over. I still had that girls' vacation coming up at Spring Break with my friends that was supposed to be a sort of bachelorette party for

Shelby's wedding at the end of the summer. I needed to think about losing a few pounds if I was going to wear a bathing suit on a sun-drenched beach.

Leaving behind the vase of flowers, I locked my house and headed out to the local animal shelter where I volunteered most Sundays. I loved animals, especially dogs, but my schedule was a nightmare and not conducive to being a responsible pet owner so I volunteered with them instead. I'd walk them, pet them, bathe them, and generally help around the shelter and then come home covered in fur and slobbering kisses.

My friends argued that I could absolutely have a dog if I wanted to. I could take it into the store with me during the day and then home with me at night. They did have a point. But I also traveled for business quite a bit and I didn't want to dump my pet on someone else to take care of. It wouldn't have been fair to them or the dog.

I did find myself weakening every now and then when a particularly adorable canine would come into the shelter. Last week we'd taken in a yellow Labrador that was about six months old, surrendered by a family that didn't realize how much work an active puppy was going to be. I'd fallen in love with "Sam" immediately when he'd looked at me with his big sad brown eyes and I had almost scooped him up then and there.

I hung up my coat in the office, giving the manager a cheery wave. "Hey, Natalie. Did you have a good Saturday?"

Tall and thin, Natalie had silver hair and a kind face. I'd known her for years, but I'd never seen her dressed up or even wearing makeup. Like every other day, she was dressed to work in old blue jeans, a sweatshirt, and boots. The only difference was today she was grinning from ear to ear and practically vibrating in her chair. Had all the animals found homes yesterday? She was positively glowing.

"This has been the best weekend ever," she gushed. "Absolutely fabulous. And you're one of the first to hear the big news. We made our donation goal for the first half of the year and then some. Isn't that amazing?"

Amazing and impossible. It was only the end of January. How on earth could we have made our six-month goal when last week we had tens of thousands to go?

"For the year?" I asked cautiously. "That does sound a little too good to be true, Nat."

Nat held out a check, her cheeks flushed with color. "But it is true. And there's more where that came from. That's just an initial donation."

I accepted the check but it fell from my nerveless fingers, fluttering onto the surface of Nat's desk. I'd taken one look at the payer and almost passed out.

He was everywhere I went. I couldn't escape.

Kyle Lewis had donated a hundred thousand dollars to the animal shelter.

"Kyle Lewis," I choked out. "That's very…generous."

The cynical part of me wondered if he was trying to buy goodwill in Arborville.

Nat, however, had no qualms about accepting the money and who could blame her? This was a small no-kill shelter with a tiny budget that operated mostly with donated labor, food, medical care, and supplies.

Nat reached out and grasped my cold hands, holding them

tightly. I could see the unshed tears in her eyes. "It's a Godsend is what it is. I didn't want to say anything, Ashlyn, but things were looking pretty dire since last fall. We didn't make our goals for the last two years. A monetary windfall from Lewis Technology will make all the difference in the world. Remember how you and I talked about trying to get corporate sponsorship?"

We had, and I'd been a huge cheerleader for that idea but now I had a sour taste in my mouth when I should be rejoicing. This wasn't about me, or Kyle, or even Natalie. This was about the animals in need and that check would make sure that they had a warm place to live, food to eat, and veterinary care until we found them a loving forever home.

I was being a selfish bitch and I didn't like myself at the moment one little bit. Everything wasn't about me and my battles.

"This is wonderful news," I said and I meant it. It *was* good news. "Did he stop by during the week?"

Her smile brightened and she clasped her hands together. "No, he's here right now and he wants to pick out a dog for adoption. I told him that I would have one of our volunteers help him. You can do that, can't you? I wouldn't trust this job to anyone else. You'll know just what to say."

I knew what to say alright, but I didn't think that was what Nat had in mind.

"Of course, I will," I heard myself responding but honestly what else could I say? It would be an opportunity for me to thank him for the flowers. Then tell him to never do that again. "I guess I'll go help him now."

So much for my fun and relaxing Sunday.

CHAPTER SEVEN

Kyle

I'D ALWAYS BELIEVED that a man made his own luck and he shouldn't wait on the universe to do him any favors. I believed in making things happen, not sitting back and waiting for life to come to me. However, I couldn't take any credit for my good luck this morning.

Ashlyn volunteered at the local animal shelter and she'd been tasked with helping me find a new furry friend. She was conflicted about it too, from what I could tell – happy that I was adopting a dog but not so happy that she was the one that had to assist me in doing it.

Me? I took it as a sign that pursuing her romantically wasn't the worst idea I'd ever had.

"What kind of dog were you looking for? Big? Small? Older? Puppy?"

We were back to the store yesterday and her stilted questioning. I was a nice guy. At least I'd been told that, and I had no reason to not believe it. People generally liked me, and I made friends easily now that I was past all that awkward teenaged nerd stuff. Ashlyn might not agree with me about the tech campus but that was only one single subject, not my whole life.

"Hi Ashlyn. It's nice to see you again."

I wasn't going to let her turn what should be a fun morning of playing with dogs into an uncomfortable few hours that we both only tolerated. The fact was she didn't know me well enough to hate me. If later she wanted to turn my photograph into a dart board I'd be supportive. Hell, I'd give her an autographed eight-by-ten glossy and a dart set.

"Kyle."

At least she hadn't called me Mr. Lewis again. But she was still standing there looking as stiff as a mannequin. What she needed was a puppy to hold. No one could stay uptight with a bouncing baby dog all up in their face.

"I'm not actually sure what I'm looking for. A dog that likes to play, I guess. Wants to go on runs with me and is active, so maybe a younger one? I don't mind training him or her."

"You've had dogs before?"

"Grew up with them but I didn't have any pets when I lived in New York City, but now I have a house and a big fenced-in yard."

Her nose had wrinkled when I mentioned the Big Apple. I'd lived there for about five years because it felt like I needed a central hub between the US and Europe, but I'd come to the conclusion a while back that I wasn't a city person. I liked wide open spaces and small towns, just like I'd grown up in. That's how I'd ended up in Arborville.

Ashlyn nodded and turned toward the main kennel doors. "Let's go then. Follow me."

It was mayhem when she opened the door. Barking dogs bellowing loud enough to bust my eardrums. The scent of hope, fear, and sadness hit my nostrils and my heart squeezed in my chest. Some of these dogs had seen some bad times.

Pick me. Pick me. If I could, I'd take them all home but the best I could do was write a big check and hope that they found families of their own. This was the best part of having a few dollars in my bank account. There sure had been a long time before when I didn't have two nickels to rub together.

Her expression immediately softening, Ashlyn knelt down next to a kennel with a small beagle inside. The dog didn't appear to be sure about what was happening but he was a happy little tyke, his tail wagging nervously as he pranced on his paws. "This is Clyde. He's a one-year-old beagle mix. He's good with kids and other dogs. He's housebroken and knows a few beginner commands. Would you like to meet him?"

I almost said yes but then out of the corner of my eye I spied inside the kennel next door. What looked to be a yellow Lab had pressed himself against the back of his cage, his head down. His entire body language was one of defeat and it made me unutterably sad to see this guy so depressed. Unlike the other dogs in this room who were barking and jumping around for attention, begging to go home with me, he'd given up.

"Who's that?"

"That's Sam," she said so softly I could barely hear her over the din. From the look on her face, she was as heartbroken about this sweet canine as I was. "He's a yellow Lab about six months old."

I scooted closer to his kennel and Sam responded by whining and trying to make himself as small as possible. "How did he get here? Was he a stray?"

There were tears in Ashlyn's eyes and she sniffled a few times. Yep, she was a softie and I couldn't help but like her all the more for it. There was something about an animal lover that I couldn't resist and this one didn't just pay lip service to it. She volunteered her scarce free time to help them. It made my check look pretty pitiful.

"He was surrendered by his family last week and he's taking it hard. They said he was too active and too much work. I have a feeling he chewed on things and wanted to play all the time. Also, he's not completely housebroken either, so he probably had accidents."

If you weren't ready for some pee and poop in your life, don't get a pet or have a baby. That was my motto and I'd learned it from my mom and dad. Wise people. Personally, cleaning up potty accidents didn't bother me. Sam was probably a great dog but thought it was all his fault that he'd been dumped here. He'd need time, patience, and love.

"I'd like to take a closer look at Sam."

★ ★ ★

Ashlyn

I CARRIED SAM'S trembling body from his kennel and into the adoption area, stroking his silky fur and trying to soothe him as best as I could. He was nervous and didn't know what was happening and my heart broke for the little pup. He was so confused, sad, and lonely. The volunteers here could only do so much for him. What he needed was a home.

The adoption area was where visitors could interact more

freely with the prospective adoptee. The room wasn't huge, about nine by nine but it had toys for the dogs to play with and some soft cushions for us to sit on. Sam, however, ignored all of the toys and simply sat where I'd placed him, on an overstuffed pillow, his wet nose tucked under a paw.

My throat clogged with emotion as Kyle immediately dropped down to the floor and simply sat by Sam, stroking his fur and crooning softly to him about what a good boy he was. He didn't try to pick him up or make Sam do anything that he wasn't ready for. They both just sat there and got to know one another while I watched.

And reevaluated Kyle Lewis.

Because anyone who could be that sweet and gentle with a scared animal wasn't the monster I thought he was. He was no Darth Vader, Joker, or Kahn. He wasn't even Eddie Haskell. He was decent man who was trying to build a building on a spot that I didn't agree with. Shelby had a point. I could like someone and not agree with them on every little thing.

"I didn't thank you for the flowers. They were beautiful."

Kyle smiled and leaned a little closer to Sam's ear. "Did you hear that, Sam? The lady liked the flowers."

"They were so exotic I didn't even know what most of them were. I think one was a tiger lily."

"It was. I'm just glad you liked them."

"I did. Thank you."

He scratched Sam behind the ear and the puppy whined, moving a little closer and placing his head on Kyle's thigh. The Lab looked up at him with those big brown eyes, so soulful and expressive. Sam recognized that this man was kind, even though the world hadn't been for the canine lately. It looked like this relationship might work out. Sam was in desperate need of love and Kyle could provide it.

"You're a good boy, aren't you? Yes, you are."

Sam was getting the idea that this situation was good, not bad. He'd crawled closer to Kyle and was now almost sitting on his lap. Kyle reached for a ball, shaking it so it made a ringing sound.

"Do you like to play, Sam?" he asked. The Lab had turned on his back for a belly rub which Kyle was happy to give. "Do you want to play ball?"

The answer was no. Sam was quite content to lie there and get his belly scratched and Ashlyn couldn't blame him. She was fascinated watching Kyle's capable hand stroke the dog's fur and imagining her own skin under those fingertips.

Stop. Just stop. This room is getting hot.

I tugged at the collar of my button-down flannel that I'd thrown on over a t-shirt. Since when did Nat keep the furnace up so high? I was roasting in here and far too young for hot flashes. My gaze landed on Kyle, who was now kissing Sam on the snout and getting licks on the cheek in return.

This is all his fault.

I might be immune to watching a man be sweet to a puppy or a baby, but my hormones weren't. He was killing me here and I couldn't take much more of it.

"So what's the verdict?"

The words came out loud. Far louder than I'd intended them to, although they would have been fine in the main kennel with a dozen barking dogs. Here in the quiet sanctuary they felt incredibly out of place. If Kyle thought I was acting strangely though, he was too well brought up to say anything. Instead, he cradled Sam's large puppy body in his arms like an infant, giving scratches behind the ear, much to the canine's delight.

"I think we've found a winner here," Kyle replied, barely able to take his eyes off of Sam. I felt a twinge of jealousy that no man had even looked at me like this one was looking at this dog, but then I gave myself an internal scolding because this was a wonderful turn of events. Sam was going to have a home. It wouldn't be my house but surely Kyle would have a good setup.

I needed to ask him a few questions before we sealed the deal, however. As a volunteer, the wellbeing of these animals was in my care and I didn't let just any Tom, Dick, or Harry come in here and adopt one.

"You said you had a big yard for Sam to play in?"

"I do. I'll need to puppy-proof the house, of course, put away my shoes and anything else he might chew but there's plenty of room for him to grow and play."

"What about when you go to work? Will someone check in on him? He's not fully grown yet and he won't be able to hold it all day yet."

"He won't be home all day alone. He'll go with me, although right now I am working from home. And to anticipate your next question, he'll travel with me if at all possible. If not, I'll get a pet sitter."

I couldn't seem to control my mouth today and the next sentence came tumbling out before I could stop it.

"Maybe your girlfriend could watch him while you travel."

Finally dragging his attention from Sam, he gave me an evil

grin. "I don't have a girlfriend. Yet."

There was admiration in his gaze and I could feel the blood rush to my cheeks and a few other places. The room had been hot before but now it was blazing. He could go from doting daddy to sex on a stick in three-point-five seconds. The man was lethal, and he was definitely aware of it.

I needed an icy blast of cool air and maybe a dunk in the frozen lake in the local park.

I reached out to give Sam a pet and at the same time Kyle moved his hand, so our fingers brushed briefly. Sparks. Lightning. Electricity. I swear that we both jumped at the contact, it was that intense.

"Well...I'll go get the paperwork for the adoption."

"Okay, should I wait here or come with you?"

I hadn't moved and my limbs didn't seem to want to.

"Uh, wait here. I'll bring the forms to you."

My legs finally took direction from my brain and I stood, my knees like jelly. It took every ounce of concentration I had to walk to the door without collapsing.

"So I'll be right back."

"Me and Sam will wait here for you."

The Lab wagged his tail upon hearing his name. He was going home. And me?

I was clearly losing my mind.

CHAPTER EIGHT

Ashlyn

K YLE'S HOME WAS a regular suburban house with a two-car garage and an expansive backyard. There were no gates at the entrance, no butler opening the door, and no cold and impersonal metal building. The furnishings were comfortable and probably expensive but not obvious and lavish. It was in a word...normal.

I hadn't planned on ever seeing his home, but when we'd finished his paperwork Nat had asked me to go with Kyle and give him a hand getting setup with his new companion. This wasn't our usual protocol, but he'd just written a six-figure check so she wanted the VIP treatment for him. Kyle hadn't realized he would find *the one* today and didn't have any supplies. So with a loaner leash and collar on Sam, the three of us stopped at the nearest pet store, practically buying out the place.

I had to admit that it was fun. Kyle immediately grabbed a cart and we filled it with a comfy dog bed, bowls, food, puppy shampoo, a brush, treats, a brand-new leash and collar, and more toys than any one dog would ever need. Sam was going crazy in the toy aisle, his tail wagging back and forth like a windshield wiper. Just seeing him this way brought tears to my eyes. He'd come out of his shell when he'd realized he had a new home and was going to get tons of love. This dog was going to be so spoiled. Just the way it should be.

Whatever toy Sam wanted, he'd received courtesy of the grinning idiot standing next to me. If I thought Sam was having a ball, it was nothing compared to Kyle. He'd appeared to be having the time of his life and the whole scene was melting the ice around my heart. A man that was this loving to an animal had to have a great deal of good inside of him.

I needed to apologize. Several times, probably. I'd let my zeal for stopping his project blind me to the fact that Kyle Lewis was a really nice guy. I should have known it before. He'd been friendly and not creepy at all in the elevator, but I'd closed my eyes to all of that. It was easier.

Kyle held up the giant dog bed. "I guess I'll put this in my bedroom. I should have grabbed two so Sam would have a place to nap in the office."

"No need." I pointed to where Sam had jumped up on the couch and had made himself at home. "He's found a comfy spot."

Kyle laughed and walked over to give the canine a cuddle. "You certainly did find a comfy spot. I don't mind you on the sofa but I'd like to at least put a blanket down so I can throw it in the wash."

"That's a good idea. Things can get a doggy smell pretty quickly."

"Make yourself at home. I'm going to put this in my bedroom."

Kyle disappeared down a hallway and that gave me a chance

to look around and be…nosy. The refrigerator was my first stop. He had a few photos stuck to the front, one with him and several people that looked to be his family. Everyone was happy, smiling, and holding ice cream cones. Kyle was a younger version of his dad but then it appeared that all the children has a strong resemblance to their parents. There were three boys and two girls and a few others that might be spouses.

The other picture was Kyle and his friend George standing on top of what looked like a mountain, grinning like idiots. Had Kyle climbed a freakin' mountain? Was there anything this man couldn't do?

"Don't be too impressed. It was a small mountain."

I whirled around to see Kyle standing behind me with a smirk on his face, Sam right by his side. He'd caught me checking out his pictures.

"You climbed a mountain?"

"Mt. Hood. It's approximately eleven thousand feet."

"That sounds big to me. I'm afraid of heights."

Kyle came closer and plucked the photo from its magnet, studying it closely. Clearly these were good memories. "It was a dare of sorts. I'd just decided not to sell some new patents and instead open my own technology business. George said we should do something to mark this occasion and I made a joke that I didn't think anything we could do would be as dumb as me opening my own business, even climbing a mountain had to be smarter. A few weeks later we did it. We did our research, of course, and it turns out Mt. Hood is good for beginners."

"Have you climbed any more mountains?"

"No, but I'd like to again. I can better understand the rush of adrenaline that people talk about."

"Do you want to climb Everest? Because people die up there."

"Yes, they do and no, I don't. I'll stick to climbs where the odds are on my side."

"Smart."

He clipped the photo back on the refrigerator and then brushed the other picture with his fingertip.

"That's my family, if you didn't already guess. We all took a vacation to St. Thomas for a week last year. What you're seeing in the photograph was literally hours before the annual Lewis Family Olympic Games. I don't like to brag but I got a gold and two bronzes."

"The Lewis Family Olympic Games?"

I had to hear about this.

"How about we get comfortable on the couch and I'll tell you all about it? I have more pictures from the events. Do you want something to drink?"

The voice in the back of my head was telling me to say no and go home. I'd done my duty for Natalie, after all. But a louder voice was telling me to say yes.

I wanted to know how he won a gold medal.

★ ★ ★

Ashlyn

AN HOUR AND a half later I'd heard all about Kyle's family, including the stories from the family Olympics through the years. It sounded like he'd had the best childhood ever.

"So your brother Paul has the most gold medals?"

"He is the oldest and he's athletically gifted. He played base-ball in college until his shoulder went."

We were sprawled on the living room floor, an almost empty pizza box sitting between us on the coffee table, and Sam draped over Kyle's lap hoping for a piece of gooey cheese or maybe a sausage bite. The puppy was looking up at his new owner with hopeful brown eyes and it looked like Kyle was going to cave.

"That's too bad. What does he do now?"

"He owns his own graphic design firm, but he still finds time to coach Little League. His team did real well last year."

"You sound proud of him."

"I am proud of him. I'm proud of all of my siblings actually, although you wouldn't have been able to tell that when we were growing up. Let's just say that the Lewis family took *sibling rivalry* to the next level. That's why my dad made up the Olympic games. I think he hoped we'd stop competing with each other on a daily basis and save it up for once a year."

"Did it work?"

Kyle took a bite out of the pizza crust. "I think it did but we're all just competitive as hell. It's in our DNA. Dad's the same and so is Mom in a much more subtle way, but sometimes I think she likes to win more than all of us put together. She's just more low-key about it."

"Your household sounds like a lot of fun. All those brothers and sisters and a house full of love."

"It's a good thing we had all of that love because that's about all we had."

"I don't understand."

"My dad was a high school physical education teacher and my mom worked part time in the school office. Those aren't exactly high-paying jobs and they had five kids. They were both only children who wanted a big family. So there was never really enough of anything. Money, food, clothes. Since I was the middle kid, I wore hand-me-downs from Paul. Poor Jack was the youngest and they were pretty worn out by the time they got to him. And let's just say that mealtime was an Olympic sport all its own. We didn't say much until we were done eating because if you snoozed you'd lose out on seconds. Between us kids and the dogs, there were never any leftovers in our house." Kyle's gaze traveled over the comfortable living room. "Things have changed, obviously."

The more I learned about this man the more shocked I was. I'd have never guessed that he'd been brought up in those circumstances. He seemed to wear the mantle of genius inventor tycoon effortlessly.

"I had no idea," I stammered, not sure what to say. "That's quite a success story. Did all of you go to college?"

"Not all of us, but we were aware that if we did we had to find our own way to pay for it. I was lucky and received several scholarships, but I still had to take out a few student loans, and of course Paul went to school on an athletic scholarship. Jack and Stacey both joined the Navy, and Kathy became a history teacher."

"Your parents must be very proud."

"I hope they are because I'm proud of them. They were terrific parents and they worked hard to give us a decent upbringing." I knew the question was coming and there was no way I could stop it. "What about you, Ashlyn? What was your childhood like?"

There it was. The one subject that I didn't want to talk about.

Crap.

CHAPTER NINE

Kyle

THE MINUTE THE question popped out of my mouth I could see that it was the wrong thing to ask. I had no idea why, of course, but I could tell that I'd stepped in it and ruined our lovely evening.

And things had been going well.

I'd watched Ashlyn turn from a nervous, uptight female into a relaxed and smiling woman who was as fun to be around as I'd imagined. This had been the best company I'd had in long time and I wanted to keep it going as long as possible. Hell, who was I kidding? I wanted to ask her out on a real date and have her say yes.

"You don't have to answer that," I said quickly when she hesitated. "It's none of my business just because I told you about mine. I have a bad habit of being nosy."

About people that I wanted to know more about. I was fascinated with Miss Ashlyn Hill and I wanted to know every single thing about her including her favorite food, movie, and band. Did she like classic rock, too?

"No, it's fine. I just don't talk about myself much, I guess. I was mostly raised by my grandmother and she always said that it's more polite to be interested in others rather than talking about ourselves. But I doubt she meant that I shouldn't answer when I'm asked."

"You don't have to answer anything. I'm not entit—"

"It's okay," Ashlyn interrupted. "I don't have any big bad secrets or anything. My life was pretty boring. I had a fairly normal childhood. No, broken bones and only one major upheaval when my mom died suddenly and I went to live with my grandmother. I did well in school, but I wasn't a genius like you. I just didn't enjoy it much. Too many cliques and I didn't fit into any of them. I was happy to graduate and go to college. There it wasn't a crime to be different."

She had my full attention now. If she'd been brought up by her grandmother that might explain her love of old things. But it was her description of herself as *different* that had my attention.

"How were you different? And I only ask because I always felt different, too. I wasn't like the other kids."

"Because you were so smart."

Yes and no.

"It was more than that. Sometimes I just felt out of step with those my own age. I wasn't a major party animal even in college. I was more serious and focused on the future."

The pizza was gone and Ashlyn flipped the top over on the box before replying. "Maybe you were focused on the future because you knew what yours might be. I think most college kids don't really and truly have a clue what they want to be when they grow up or how to create a secure future for themselves. It's kind of ridiculous, don't you think, that we ask eighteen-year-olds to pick what they want to be and do for the rest of their lives? Only a few know and we've barely experienced life at eighteen. I've always said that I don't think kids should be allowed to go to college until they're twenty-one. They should have to live and work for a few years and see what they're good at."

Her cheeks had gone quite pink and she buried her face in her hands. "I am so sorry. I really climbed up on my soapbox, didn't I? I'll shut up now."

Tentatively reaching out, I gently pulled her hands away from her face. She'd never invited me to touch her before, but she didn't shy away or slap my face. It was progress.

"I think you've made a valid point. Some of my friends are in far different fields now than their majors. Your idea has merit."

Ashlyn ruffled Sam's fur and scratched behind the dog's ears. I was now officially jealous of my own pet. "Except for you. You knew what you wanted to do."

"In a way. I wanted to make a difference and I wanted to make enough money to pay off my student loans and get a decent car. Not exactly the loftiest of goals." It occurred to me in that moment that Ashlyn might not agree that I had attained those targets. To her I was a killer of old homes. "I know that you and I don't agree on my new project, but this is something I've been wanting to do for years. It's the culmination of a dream."

She sucked in a breath and seemed to be weighing her words carefully. I took it as a good sign that she didn't want to insult or upset me. "I don't have an argument against your dream, Kyle. My only battle is where you've chosen to build it. I think there are other, better places."

"I hope to convince you differently."

Because I liked this woman. A whole hell of a lot. I wanted to see where things might go with her, but this development project sat right between us just waiting to throw a spanner in the works.

"I've done my homework."

She had but only up to a point.

"You have put a great deal of effort into this, but please believe me when I say that I've crossed every t and dotted every 'i' for this project. This is my dream, remember? Half-measure simply wouldn't do. This may be the most important thing I've ever done in my life. If you're interested I can have some of the reports sent to you so you can read them for yourself. I'm an open book on my method here and I'm willing to let you see it all." I leaned forward so that she could see into my eyes. I wanted her to see the truth there. "What are your dreams, Ashlyn?"

I thought that perhaps I'd crossed another line, but her gaze went a little dreamy and soft and then she sighed softly, sort of shrugging as if whatever had passed through her intelligent brain didn't matter.

"I wanted to have my own business and now I do."

Was that it? From her expression I didn't think so.

"Is that it?"

Her brows flew up and she gave me a disbelieving look. "Isn't that enough?"

"It is," I assured her, deciding to be brave and placing my hand on hers where it rested on the rug. Her skin was warm and soft and I couldn't stop myself from wondering if she was like that all over. My imagination was always getting me in trouble. "It's an amazing dream. I just wondered if you had others."

"Well...I want to be happy. But I think everyone does so I'm not sure that it's a dream."

"What about a family? Would you like that?"

A supremely personal question but I'd gone ahead and asked it. Something flashed behind her eyes, but it was gone in an instant.

"Maybe. If I found the right person."

I had definitely hit a nerve but our first evening wasn't the time to probe at it. I didn't know what past hurts I'd be bringing up. Clearly though, there was more to Ashlyn Hill than what she put out there to the world and I wanted to know every detail. If she'd been hurt in the past I wanted to kiss and make it better.

"Ashlyn, do you like music?"

I'd surprised her by not pursuing my previous line of questioning and she blinked a few times as if processing my words.

"I do. Very much."

I grinned and raised her hand so I could press my lips to her knuckles. "Then may I have this dance, Miss Hill?"

Luckily, I was well used to people looking at me like I had a screw loose. It had been happening my entire life. "You want to *dance?*"

"Yes. I think we should show Sam how it's done."

The snoozing canine raised his head at hearing his name and nudged my hand for more pets. I was happy to oblige.

"You want to dance?" she asked again. "Right now?"

"I can't think of a better time. What kind of music do you

like?" I rose and tugged her to her feet. If she liked the past, I had just the thing. My aunt had taught me and my siblings when we were kids. "Have you ever done the Hustle?"

★ ★ ★

Ashlyn

BY THE TIME we fell in a heap on the sofa, giggling like teenagers and more than a little sweaty, I knew I was in big trouble. I could fall hard for a man like this, but we were so different. Could any sort of relationship between us survive?

I doubted it. One of us would end up with a broken heart and it would probably be me. Frankly, I was tired of being the one crying after a breakup while my friends brought over ribs and ice cream, telling me he wasn't worth it.

Sam had almost tripped us up, dancing around our legs with his tail wagging a mile a minute and thumping against the cushions on the couch. He was a far cry from the sad little puppy he'd been only this morning and my throat clogged with emotion again at the thought of the life he was going to have now. The puppy jumped up on us, his paws digging into our stomachs and knocking the wind from our lungs even as we struggled to catch our breath. Kyle quickly scooped the dog up in his arms and scratched him on the belly, much to Sam's delight.

"Woman, you wore me out. I haven't danced like that since my sister's wedding last year."

Slapping my hand over my mouth, I tried to hold in my laughter. "Did you win the gold in dancing?"

"Naw, Jack would win hands down. I'm a little too awkward to medal in that event. You, on the other hand, would blow the competition out of the water. You're amazing. Did you take lessons or is it natural?"

Blushing all the way to the roots of my hair, I shook my head. "No lessons. I just like music."

Another thing Kyle and I had in common besides dogs. He had music on his phone, but he also had a vinyl collection that was impressive. Not as large as my own, of course. I'd also caught sight of some of his DVDs on a bookshelf and there were some old black and whites along with newer titles.

"Me too," he said, his voice husky and low. We were sitting side by side, his thigh pressed against mine and I could smell the citrusy aroma of his body wash mixed with his own scent that was very pleasant indeed. Sort of warm and comfortable. Like a soft sweater in the fall. "I'm glad you came over to help me with Sam."

Our gazes locked and I couldn't help but stare into his brown eyes. His pupils were blown wide and if I'd looked in a mirror I was sure mine would be the same. "I am, too."

"You know what might be even more fun? If you let me take you out on a date." He leaned down more closely so I could feel his warm breath on my cheek. "I'm a decent man, Ashlyn. Let me prove it to you."

"You don't have to. I can see it. I'm sorry I've been such a bitch. It's just—"

His fingertip pressed against my lips and a zing of electricity ran through my body straight down to my toes. I couldn't remember the last time I'd reacted this strongly to a simple touch.

"You don't have to apologize. I understand your passion."

He did but… Those houses were still slated to be demolished. He had a point about how much money it would take to restore them, though. Few had that sort of wealth.

"Do you want to think about it?" he asked, pulling back. Even Sam seemed to withdraw slightly as if he could feel the tension between us. "I don't want to push you into something you're not sure about."

I wasn't sure, and I had a feeling that I might vacillate back and forth, sort of twisting in the wind at the rate I was going. What would Shelby say about this?

Make a damn decision and own it. I needed to either say yes or forget Kyle Lewis even existed. I wasn't necessarily ready to do the former, but I was positive I couldn't do the latter. That left me only one option.

"Yes, I'll go out with you."

A leap of faith. What could possibly go wrong?

CHAPTER TEN

Kyle

S O MUCH FOR the doggy bed. Sam slept with me which I didn't mind. He sprawled at the foot of the bed for most of the night and then woke me up bright and early for breakfast and a morning pee. It was a good thing I was an early riser because the sun was barely over the horizon when he'd licked my face and hands to wake me up. Of course, after I'd let him run around in the backyard and fed him, he came inside and curled up on the couch for a nap.

George showed up a few hours later with two coffees and a box of donuts that had Sam wide awake and sniffing the air. I'm definitely the type that will give a dog some people food but a glazed donut? No way. He could have a chicken and apple treat from the pet store.

"Looks like you got yourself a new roommate." George leaned down to ruffle Sam's fur and received a lick on the hand in return.

"This is Sam and it appears that he likes you. No accounting for taste, I guess."

George held up the box of donuts. "I think I know why I'm one of his favorite people. When these are all gone I might not be held in such high regard."

"He'll remember," I assured my friend. "He hasn't been here long but already I can tell he's highly motivated by food."

George set the box and coffee on the kitchen counter. "Aren't we all? The chocolate frosted are for me so keep your grubby mitts off of them."

I can't count how many times my friend had said those exact words to me every single time we had a box of donuts sitting between us. By now I knew that if I reached for a chocolate frosted, I'd be taking my life into my hands. Besides, my favorite were the custard cream-filled, and there was no better way to celebrate getting Ashlyn to say yes to a date than eating a sugar-filled concoction that wasn't good for me.

I shoved one into my mouth, taking a huge bite. I'd have to run a half marathon to burn off these calories. "I don't even want your chocolate donuts so relax. You're far too tense. You should do something about that. Meditate. Get a massage. Go for a walk in nature."

"Screw you," George said, his mouth full. "I'm not stressed, just protective. And why are you so chill? I've heard that having a pet lowers your blood pressure, but they didn't say that it would make you grin like the Joker. It's slightly disturbing."

I swallowed the last bite of donut. "I'll have you know that I officially have a date with Miss Ashlyn Hill. I'm taking her to dinner and a movie tomorrow night."

That was the plan, anyway. I'd picked out a nice restaurant and one of the movie theaters on campus was showing a Hitchcock double feature. I hoped that Ashlyn's love of the past included *Rear Window* and *Vertigo*.

"An official date? As compared to an unofficial one?"

"Last night was sort of an unofficial date. She helped me with Sam. Turns out she volunteers at the animal shelter."

"That's some grade A universe shit. Like something out of a movie. You really didn't know she was a volunteer there?"

I didn't but if I had I would have adopted Sam days earlier.

"I think I was as shocked to see her as she was to see me. But she hung out here for awhile and it was great. She's…terrific."

What a fucking lame word. I couldn't even describe how much I liked her and how incredibly attracted to her I was. And I was supposed to be a genius. Around Ashlyn though, I felt like I was back in high school with a crush on the prom queen.

"Well, don't fuck it up. That's my advice."

George was always full of wisdom, some of it better than others.

"I'm not planning to."

"You weren't planning on getting stuck in that elevator the other night, but shit happens, my friend. Be ready. Wine her, dine her, and impress the fuck out of her." He leaned forward, placing his palms on the marble countertop. "But whatever you do, do not under any circumstances talk about the tech campus with this woman. I know you're all excited but I'm telling you…don't do it. Nothing good can come from it. Avoid that topic at all costs."

That might just be the best advice George had ever given me.

Ashlyn

MONDAY IS MY day off and that's when I do my errands and chores. I'd woken up early and straightened the house before heading off to the grocery store to pick up food for the week. Later it was off to yoga class where I was meeting Emmy and Shelby when they finished work.

After some sun salutations and forty-five minutes of stretching my body into several ridiculous positions, the three of us found ourselves back at the barbecue joint for dinner. The waitress had barely left the table before Shelby was hounding me with the one question I didn't want her to ask.

"Have you finished the book yet?"

Well…no.

"I'm working on it," I said instead. "I've just been so busy this week."

Which was totally the truth. Shelby, however, was crestfallen, her lips dropping at the corners as if I'd just told her Santa Claus wasn't real and neither was the Easter Bunny.

"Oh. I guess I was hoping it would be the kind of book a person couldn't put down."

Crap, now I'd hurt her feelings and that was the last thing I'd wanted to do. She was one of my three best friends in the whole world and now she felt like shit because I hadn't finished reading her book.

"It's a great book. I've just really been busy. I'm going to finish it tonight."

There. I'd made the commitment. Now I had to do it. The

fact was I was finding some of Shelby's advice a little old-fashioned, although Emmy had assured me that Mia had said the same thing. Supposedly the book would get much, much better if I stuck with it.

Shelby's eyes lit up. "That's wonderful. You can call me anytime day or night to ask questions if you need to."

"I don't think I'll need to do that but thank you for the offer."

"Now we just need to find you a man to practice on," Emmy said. "Too bad you turned down Kyle Lewis."

About that...

I took a sip of my tea and then cleared my throat. "Funny you mention Kyle. He came to the animal shelter yesterday and adopted a dog – the yellow Lab Sam. I think I mentioned him last week. Anyway, Natalie asked me to give Kyle a hand with shopping for supplies and getting Sam situated in his new home."

Emmy grinned and clapped her hands together. "Sam has a new home? That's wonderful news."

Shelby shot Emmy a dirty look. "That's what you got from that? Sam has a new home. How about Ashlyn gave Kyle Lewis help?" She turned back to me, her eyes wide with excitement. "Did you go to his house? What's it like? Is everything voice-activated? Does he really have a self-driving car?"

I wasn't sure which question to answer first so I answered them all. One by one.

"I did go to his house and it's a very nice but normal ranch in a normal neighborhood. I have no idea if everything or anything is voice-activated but he didn't talk to the refrigerator or the microwave. As for the car, he drove it himself, but I guess he could have a second one in the garage. I didn't check."

Emmy rolled her eyes and elbowed Shelby. "You didn't ask the most important question. What happened?"

I truly wanted their advice but admitting that I'd given in wasn't easy.

"I caved."

★ ★ ★

Ashlyn

"IT'S GOING TO be fine. I'll bet you have a great time."

That was from Emmy after I'd told the entire story of how I found myself with a date the next night with none other than Kyle Lewis. He was supposed to be my sworn enemy and now he might end up being my boyfriend.

If things worked out. If last night was anything to go by, they would.

"That's exactly what I'm afraid of."

Shelby and Emmy frowned, exchanging a puzzled look.

"What exactly are you afraid of?" Shelby asked. "And be specific."

"That we'll have a good time." Couldn't they see it? "That would be a problem."

Emmy placed her fork on the edge of her plate and daintily dabbed at her mouth with her paper napkin. "Help me here. How would having a good time on your date be a problem?"

I was going to have to explain it in detail to two of the smartest women I knew.

"If we have a good time, then he's probably going to ask me out again."

Shelby nodded. "True. Keep going…"

"If he asks me out again, I'll probably say yes. So there will be a second date."

Emmy giggled and slapped her hand over her mouth. "This is like that book with the mouse and the cookie. Let me guess how this story ends. You keep dating and it's fantastic. You have sex and it's the best ever. Then you fall in love and end up getting married to a man who loves technology. Am I right?"

I threw up my hands I frustration. "You don't think that would be an issue?"

"Maybe you should see how this first date goes," Shelby said. "Then decide if your coupling with Kyle Lewis would bring about a tragic dystopian future for all mankind."

"I had fun last night," I whispered begrudgingly. "A lot of fun. There was…chemistry."

Both my friends' mouths were shaped in perfect "O's", but it was Emmy who found her voice first.

"Heat between you two. I'm not surprised after your encounter in the elevator. Wouldn't it have been wild if you'd been stuck for hours and ended up having sex with him right then and there?"

"No, that would not have been wild," I hissed, my cheeks growing warm at the thought. Kyle was sexy as hell and the image of him pressing me back against the wall while my legs were wrapped around his waist had me squirming in my chair. I'd always heard that a man that could dance well was probably also a good lover. Kyle could dance. He could definitely move those hips. "There might be cameras in that elevator. I don't want to end up on the internet."

"So you think this relationship might go somewhere?" Shelby asked, excitement in her tone. She was practically bouncing up and down in her chair. "Then it's even more important to read the book before your date."

"She's already trapped the man," Emmy pointed out. "Now she just has to decide whether she wants to keep him."

"The book talks about that," Shelby replied smugly. "It's not just about getting asked out. It's a complete relationship manual. Which you would know if you'd read it."

Emmy held up her hands in surrender. "Fine. Okay. No need to get snippy. I'll read it after Ashlyn."

"I'm not snippy. I'm just nervous. I have a lot going on with the wedding preparations."

"You are a little snippy," Emmy said, holding up one finger. "And you get a day. One day. Don't think you can use that excuse all the way until August. We're your friends and we will call you out."

Emmy was an event planner and she did a truckload of weddings. She'd made it her mission not to let Shelby become some sort of monster bride.

"Fine," Shelby huffed. "I'm just trying to help Ashlyn."

"Then help me decide if I should call him back and call off the whole date," I said, burying my face in my hands. "I've never been this nervous before a date. He's not like the guys I usually date."

"Thank goodness," Emmy breathed dramatically. "You are far too into tortured artists and guys that can't afford their electric bill. It's okay to be attracted to a successful man who has his shit together and isn't suffering for his art."

That had been my go-to type for a long time but after my last ex-boyfriend I'd vowed to make a change. Apparently, I hadn't been specific, though, because the universe had sent me Kyle. Wow, was he different.

"What happens if I fall for Kyle? How could we make this work?"

Emmy picked up her fork and dug into her chicken. "I'm not sure how it would work but there is one thing I'm sure of."

"What's that?"

"If you're asking that question…it's too late. You've already fallen."

Damn. She was probably right.

CHAPTER ELEVEN

Kyle

I HADN'T BEEN this nervous about a date in years. If ever. So much was riding on this one evening and I couldn't afford even a small misstep. In my work, I didn't mind mistakes; in fact, I embraced them because they brought me closer to the real solution. But Ashlyn wasn't a computer program or a piece of electronics.

She was breathtakingly gorgeous.

Or at least I thought she was when she opened the door the next evening. Dressed in a sapphire blue sweater dress and brown boots, she'd pulled her long blonde hair up in some sort of bun on the top of her head with silky tendrils hanging around her face. I had an almost overwhelmingly urge to reach over and pull out the hairpins holding it in place, but I managed to restrain myself. Barely.

Ashlyn looked up at me from under her lashes, a little shy and a little sexy. My heart lurched in my chest and then went off at a gallop. "Hi."

"Hi."

She stepped back slightly, the door opening wider. "Do you...do you want to come in for a minute? I just need some lipstick and my purse and then we can go."

Did I want to come in? Hell yes, I wanted to come in. What I really wanted was to sweep her off of her feet and carry her into her bedroom – wherever it was – and spend the rest of the night making love to her. But that wasn't going to happen. I was going to be good and act like a goddamn gentleman if it killed me. My caveman instincts would be ignored, at least until they were welcome and invited.

I entered her home and inhaled a lungful of her scent. It was everywhere and if my heart wasn't thumping loudly enough for the whole town to hear before it definitely was now.

The inside of Ashlyn's condo was everything the outside wasn't. Personal and cozy. There were framed black and white photos on the walls along with a few bright paintings here and there. Colorful throw pillows and a beautiful quilt were draped over the end of her cream-colored sofa, and in one corner was a lovely old wooden rocker. There were candles everywhere and two brass sconces on the wall flanking a large set of floor to ceiling shelves filled with books, DVDs, board games, and albums. A turntable was tucked into a corner of the room.

"How do you reach the top shelf?"

The question popped into my head and out of my mouth before I could stop it. It wasn't a terrible question, though. Ashlyn was petite, and those shelves had to be about eight feet tall. I'd be stretching to reach the top.

She pointed to a blue velvet ottoman. "I stand on that and reach as high as I can."

"That sounds incredibly dangerous."

Retrieving a gold tube of lipstick from her purse, she peered into a mirror above the table by the door.

"Luckily, I rarely need anything from the top shelf, but it's sweet that you're worried for my safety. I can assure you that the ottoman is sturdy."

The relative safety of living room furniture had been completely dashed from my mind as I watched – mesmerized – as Ashlyn applied her lipstick. It was one of the most erotic acts I'd seen, and I had no doubt it wasn't meant to be in the least. She was simply putting on lipstick and my body was reacting as if she was doing a striptease dance just for me. Every nerve in my body had stood up and taken notice as she'd glided that tube of color – so slowly and sensually – over her full lips.

My nasty, dirty mind had already conjured up an image of those red lips wrapped around my cock, and he was agreeing that this was a desirable thing to do. He was pressing against my fly and I had to shift so that my jacket covered my crotch. I didn't want her to know just how debauched I could actually be. Better that she find that out later.

Unable to form coherent words, I hadn't replied to her statement, but she was done putting on lipstick and seemed to be watching me, expecting me to say something. I mentally smacked myself in the head and pasted on my best *I'm not a pervert* smile.

"Ready to go?"

The cold air outside would do me good.

Ashlyn

THE DATE WAS going better than I thought it would. Which was saying something because I'd had more than a remote inkling that we would have a good time together. All through dinner he'd regaled me with tales of growing up with so many siblings, his college years, and then when he'd started his own business. He was a self-made man but extremely humble, giving credit to just about everyone in his life but himself.

Dammit, he was even more attractive than before. All through dinner I'd barely been able to drag my gaze from him. He was dressed in casual slacks and a button-down shirt but somehow on him the ordinary looked…extraordinary. The seams strained at his wide shoulders and the buttons outlined a path directly from his chest down to…

Stop. Just stop. I was rather horrified by the turn my thoughts had taken. Images of Kyle without that conservative white shirt were trying to take over my usually orderly brain. I couldn't seem to drag my gaze from his lips as he spoke and his hands were suddenly fascinating, the way they worked his knife and fork. Clearly, I needed to call Shelby and make an appointment for deep therapy.

We'd carefully avoided the elephant sitting nonchalantly in the corner. His technical campus. He'd already told me it was his dream and after hearing his journey I wanted him to have it. Was it terrible that I simply wanted him to have it someplace else?

A few times I thought about talking to him about it, but the evening was going so well I didn't want to ruin it. We were having fun, the food was delicious, and the service was excellent. Why mess with it? We weren't going to agree, and it was going to make the date end up in a huge catastrophe.

With things going that well, it had lulled me into a false sense of security. I should have expected it, prepared for it, but somehow I'd fooled myself that it would never happen.

He asked it over dessert – a decadent chocolate cake that had my taste buds singing. We were sharing a slice.

"So tell me about your grandmother, Ashlyn. You said she raised you, correct?"

I might as well get it over with. Rip that band-aid off as fast as possible.

"She did. My mother passed away when I was ten and I went to live with Gran. I guess you could say that's where I get my love of the past from. She likes to collect records and funny novelty items. She also loves books and she must have hundreds of them."

A frown flickered across his handsome features but then he smiled. "She's alive? For some reason I thought she had passed on. I guess I haven't been paying attention. Sorry about that."

"I never said, so it's fine. You may have thought that because she doesn't live near here anymore, so I don't see her as much as I'd like to."

And here it comes…

"Where does she live now?"

I took a deep breath. "Washington D.C."

"That's quite a difference, Central Illinois to the nation's capital."

"She moved there for work."

"She's not retired? That's wonderful. What does she do?"

I swallowed the cake in my mouth that had turned dry as sawdust. "She's a senator."

Kyle blinked once, then twice, then a third time. "A senator? You mean like a U.S. senator and that domed building?"

"The very one," I said with a sigh. "I usually don't talk about Gran at the beginning of a relationship because, frankly, things can get a little heated when it comes to politics. She's a lightning rod for controversy and she's extremely outspoken. For some reason, that seems to upset the men I've dated."

Kyle stroked his chin and grinned. "I'm afraid to ask this question but who is your grandmother?"

"Roslyn Caldwell."

The look on his face would have been comical if it had been anyone else. His eyes widened and his mouth fell open. Then he started laughing. I wasn't sure if that was a good sign or a bad one.

"Your grandmother is Senator Roslyn Caldwell? What an amazing woman. You must be very proud."

I was, actually, although Kyle probably thought that I wasn't.

"I am very proud. She's always fought for what she believes in even if it wasn't popular. She's in her seventies but she has more energy than most teenagers I know."

Growing up as her granddaughter had been a challenge. For so many reasons that didn't have a thing to do with politics. Because of her career, I didn't have what many would consider a normal childhood. She was always taking me to marches, rallies, and I'd worked on my first political campaign stuffing envelopes when I was thirteen. Gran had been passionate about changing the world and she'd made me that way, too.

"She was on CNN last night talking about a housing bill."

"I didn't know that but she's on those shows quite a bit."

"You take after her."

I took a sip of my water as my throat tightened. He didn't know how much that compliment meant to me. Despite the challenging nature of my relationship with Gran, I loved her terribly. "Thank you."

"You really are," he pressed. "Look at you fighting at city hall for your beliefs. I bet your grandmother used to do that, too."

"She did. A lot better than me."

Gran had usually won her fights.

"I bet you do just fine."

"Not this time."

The words tumbling out of my mouth before I could stop myself and I wanted to reach out and snatch them back, but it was far too late. I'd opened up the subject that we'd both been avoiding.

Reaching across the table, Kyle placed his hand over mine, tangling the fingers together. "You did really good, Ashlyn. I wish I could save those houses, and it might have been possible twenty years ago, but it's just too late for them. Give me something else to save for you and I'll do it. Some trees? A lake? An endangered species? I'll be all over it. I just can't fix this one thing."

My throat clogged at his earnest expression. He was totally serious and not making fun of me in any way.

"I know," I finally said, folding my napkin on the table but leaving my other hand in his. It felt too good to pull away. "I'm trying to be okay with it but it's hard. Isn't it about time to go to the movie? I love Hitchcock."

I didn't want to talk about it anymore. I just wanted to enjoy myself with Kyle.

"I don't want this to come between us, Ashlyn. I really like you and I think we could be good together."

"I really like you, too."

Denying it was useless.

Kyle's smile widened and he waggled his eyebrows playfully. "You just want me for my dog. Admit it."

"He is pretty handsome. And sweet."

Shaking his head, Kyle sighed. "I guess a guy has to have a wet nose and fur to get some love around here."

"It wouldn't hurt."

His smile grew wider. "I could lick your cheek. You like it when Sam does it."

I would definitely like it. In fact, I liked just about everything when it came to Kyle Lewis.

I was falling hard and fast, and I was enjoying every minute of it.

CHAPTER TWELVE

Ashlyn

WE HAD WATCHED the first half of the double feature, *Rear Window*, but *Vertigo* wasn't my favorite and we were both fidgeting in our seats by the time the credits rolled. By mutual decision we decided to forgo the second film and head home.

The car ride back to my condo was quiet, just the soft hum of the heater in the background and the sound of the tires on the road. The tension between us had begun to build the moment I stepped into the vehicle and had continued to grow the closer we came to our destination. An unspoken question was hanging between us...

Would I invite Kyle in?

If I didn't invite him in, it didn't mean that the date wasn't great. It had been quite good, and I hoped he'd asked me out again. It simply meant that the evening was over and I was going to my house and he should leave and go to his. There was nothing bad about that.

But...

If I did invite him in, it also didn't mean that I was inviting him for sex. I could simply be inviting him in for hot chocolate and more stimulating conversation. Maybe a kiss or two. It didn't have to mean that we were definitely going to be intimate. I simply didn't want the evening to end so early.

I wasn't a prude and I was far from a virgin. I didn't have any weird hangups regarding sex and I adored having an orgasm, especially when I didn't have to do it all myself. But I wasn't the type to jump into bed with someone the minute I met them. I had to have more than a mere physical attraction; I wanted an emotional and intellectual one, too.

The problem was I had it. I was more connected to Kyle in a week of knowing him than I had been with my last boyfriend of four months. And it scared me to death.

Because if this blew up in my face, I'd care far more than I had in a damn long time. It was going to hurt.

Dammit, I should have finished Shelby's book last night, but I'd been exhausted and had fallen asleep watching a mystery show on Netflix right before the reveal of whodunnit. The book might have been able to give me some advice to traverse this delicate terrain, but I was out here on my own and nervous as hell. Screw the hot chocolate. I needed a glass of wine. Or a shot of whiskey.

I didn't have much longer to ponder the question, however. Kyle pulled into my driveway and cut the engine, bounding out of the car before I had a chance to say anything. He opened my door and held out a hand. I placed mine in his and let him help me from the low-slung vehicle. He didn't have a sports car as I'd expected but the two-door coupe was clearly expensive, smelling of leather and...Kyle.

"Safely home," he murmured in my ear as he escorted me to

the door. The air between us practically crackled with electricity and I was sure that if I touched his skin a spark would fly into the air. This was it. The goodnight kiss. I'd been thinking about it since I'd accepted his invitation. I couldn't help but wonder how his lips would feel and taste. I did have a feeling that he would be good at it. I'd learned that he was the kind of man that liked to master a skill. He would be an excellent kisser. And lover.

Unbidden thoughts – all of them sexual – flooded my filthy mind and every hormone in my body stood up and took notice. It had been awhile since I'd had a man in my house, let alone in my bed. Did I want this one there?

I fumbled in my purse for the house key and finally held it up in triumph. "Found it."

I'd left the porch light on so I could see the door, but my trembling fingers weren't cooperating. I couldn't seem to get the darn thing in the lock.

"Let me help you."

Gently, Kyle took the key ring from my nerveless fingers and easily unlocked the door with a loud click.

"There you go."

"Thank you."

Why did I sound so breathless? As if I'd run a marathon? Oh, right. Because I was nervous as hell and acting like a schoolgirl on my first date. Kyle was only a man. A normal, ordinary guy who happened to be smarter than most and have more money. Sure, he was handsome and sexy but there were lots of men out in the world like that. Probably. I hadn't met many, but I didn't get out much.

Note to self. Socialize more. Work less. Get a life. Ask Shelby to write a book about work life balance.

That didn't help me right now, though.

I took a deep breath and looked up at Kyle. "Thank you for the lovely evening. I had a wonderful time."

"I did, too. We should do this again."

"We should—"

I was going to say more but then his fingers brushed my cheek, sucking the oxygen from my lungs. He bent his head as his hand cupped my jaw and softly pressed his warm lips to mine. My mouth instantly parted, and whether it was to breathe in more air or to invite his tongue I didn't know, but it had the same effect. His hand snaked around the back of my head and the kiss became more seeking, and a hell of lot more passionate. I clung to the sleeves of his coat as the world spun around me. By the time he lifted his head, I was shocked that there was still snow on my front lawn. It had to be ninety degrees at least and it felt like July instead of January.

"I've been thinking about that all night," he admitted, his mouth hovering mere millimeters above my own. He stole a quick kiss once more, the tip of his tongue running along my bottom lip and sending shivers up my spine. "It was better than I ever imagined."

Yes. Yes, it was.

There were a million reasons not to do it, but I couldn't think of even one. Later I'd come to my senses.

I placed my hand on the doorknob. "Do you want to come inside for a glass of wine?"

★　★　★

Kyle

FUCK YES, I wanted to come inside. I wanted to keep kissing Ashlyn until our clothes magically fell off and we ended up in her bed. I'd keep her there for days if she'd let me. There were so many naughty things I wanted to do to her.

Whoa.

I need to slow down. Ashlyn had invited me in for a glass of wine, not a wild fuck on her kitchen counter. I'd do well to remember that and behave or I might find myself shoved out into the snow after being smacked across the face.

As my dad used to say, "Don't count your chickens, son. And what that means is don't think she's thinking the same thing you are. Unless she grabs your crotch and drags you into the bedroom. Then maybe, just maybe, she's saying yes."

This was a glass of wine and some conversation. Some cuddles and kisses, too, if I had my way. I'd let her know I was interested and then put the ball in her court…

Ashlyn took my coat and draped it over a chair but wouldn't make eye contact with me. I could tell at the door she was nervous, but it seemed to have gone up a few rungs since she'd invited me inside. Was she regretting it?

"I have a really nice cabernet," she said, retrieving a bottle from a wine rack tucked next to her pantry. I'd followed her into the kitchen but she still wasn't paying any attention to me, intent on grabbing two wine glasses on a shelf out of her reach.

"Let me get those for you."

I'd come up behind and reached over her head, her pert little bottom pressed against me for a few seconds.

"Here you go." I set the two glasses on the counter and eased away, giving her some space. "Do you want me to open the wine?"

"Yes, that would be nice. Thank you."

She sounded so prim and proper. So polite. I quickly dispatched the corkscrew and poured us each half a glass. I didn't need the alcohol and I didn't want her decision making impaired either.

"Do you want to watch some television?" Ashlyn slipped out of the kitchen and now had the remote in her hand. "We could watch a movie."

Except that's exactly what we'd left fifteen minutes ago. I had another idea. Hopefully one that would get rid of all this nervousness.

"Why don't we turn on some music?"

I wanted to dance with Ashlyn.

CHAPTER THIRTEEN

Ashlyn

MUSIC SOUNDED LIKE a good idea. I was so nervous I was beginning to sweat, and music always calmed me down. It occurred to me that Kyle might be nervous as well since he'd suggested it. It was kind of nice not to be alone in this.

Flipping through my album collection, I paused at Van Morrison's "Moondance". It was one of my favorites. Kyle had shown that he was into music from the past...

"I love that song." So lost in thought, I hadn't heard Kyle come up behind me. He tapped the album cover. "If you're contemplating playing that I'm completely on board."

Decision made. Within seconds the classic album from 1970 was playing on my turntable.

Kyle's arm went around my waist, pulling me back against him. "Dance with me."

I liked dancing, but I wasn't the greatest. I had rhythm, but I lacked really cool moves.

"Um..."

Leaning down, he whispered in my ear, his breath warm against my cheek. "Please."

I dare anyone to say no to that. I couldn't. So I let him lead me out to the center of my living room floor where he lifted my arms so they were around his neck and his hands were on my hips. Our bodies were so close I could feel the heat of his skin and smell the tangy scent of his aftershave.

Our first movements were rather awkward but then we seemed to find our rhythm, and we danced together as if we'd been doing it for years. I couldn't help but giggle as he playfully twirled me around, our bodies brushing as he pulled me close again. I'd read about the mating dances of animals, but this was the first time I'd actually participated in one.

I could feel the warmth in my cheeks. I was blushing a bright red. I always did when I was aroused, and I couldn't help it unless I dunked my head in a bucket of ice water, which I wasn't going to do. Kyle was going to have a pretty big clue as to what he was doing to me and I was just going to have to live with that. I didn't mind too much, actually. I could feel his own arousal pressing against my hip. We both had the same idea.

But I wasn't the type of person to do every single thing I wanted to. I wanted to eat ice cream for dinner, but I usually didn't do it.

I was definitely attracted to Kyle. He was handsome, sexy, funny, smart, and kind. I'd grown to like him. A whole bunch. I also wasn't a prude. If I wanted to make love to a man I didn't need to go back and forth about whether to do it. I owned my sexuality and I didn't regret it in the morning. But I'd been around this block enough times to know that going to bed with someone changed things. It made it more... It just made it more. At least to me it did. It might not to him, but I didn't go around jumping into bed with people on a whim.

While I'd been thinking about whether to sleep with Kyle, the song had ended and we were standing in the middle of my small living room. My hands were still holding his and we were standing close. Oh, so close. Looking up at him from under my lashes, I could see him smiling. His eyes has a soft unfocused look to them, but it was his face that pushed me across the line.

His cheeks had taken on a ruddy color. Just like mine.

★ ★ ★

GLIDING MY HANDS up over his wide shoulders, I looped my arms around Kyle's neck, pulling him down for a kiss. Our first kiss.

Hot and sweet and lingering. He didn't shove his tongue between my lips but instead finessed his way in, swiping at my lower lip and nibbling at the corner of my mouth. He took his time, seemingly content to explore, his hands running down my sides and coming to rest on my hips as his lips caressed mine. By the time he lifted his head, we were both breathless and my knees had gone weak. I was clinging to him for support.

"That was…amazing," he murmured, somehow managing to bring me closer. I could feel the buttons on his shirt and the press of his belt buckle. "Just amazing."

"I think so, too."

It was only the two of us. The outside world had disappeared, and it was just Kyle and myself. There were so many reasons to care about this man and a few reasons not to. They didn't seem all that important anymore. I'd seen the good in

Kyle.

"I guess…I should be going home."

There was hesitation in his voice, a question that hung in the air. How would I answer it? He was leaving this up to me. I would have to be explicit in my consent and affirmation. He wasn't going to make another move without an invitation.

"You could," I replied, my own voice sounding husky and unfamiliar. My fingers played with the soft material of his shirt. "Or you could stay awhile longer. If you wanted to."

He leaned down and pressed his forehead to mine. "I want to be with you, Ashlyn. I need to hear you say you want that, too. If you don't, that's fine. I get it. We haven't known each other very long and you might–"

"Iwanttobewithyoutoo."

The words tumbled out of my mouth so quickly they ran together, and I wasn't sure if he would even understand what I'd said.

I hadn't realized I'd been holding my breath until I saw the slow smile that crossed his face.

"Are you sure, Ashlyn? I don't want there to be any regrets in the morning."

"I'm sure," I said because I *was* sure. "No regrets."

The world slowed down just for us. There was no hurry into the bedroom. In fact, I wasn't sure how we even managed to get there between the kissing and the touching.

When we both stood at the foot of my bed with just the small bedside lamp for light, I should have felt shy and self-conscious, but I didn't. I couldn't. Not with the way he was looking at me. His gaze admiring from the top of my head to the tip of my toes. If anything, it made me bold and confident and I tossed aside the outer layer of clothes as if I stripped in front of a horny male all the time. No big deal. I paused, however, when I was down to my bra and panties. He hadn't shed any of his garments yet and I didn't want to be naked while he was fully dressed.

"You're so gorgeous," he said, his voice hoarse with want and need. I could recognize it because I had no doubt that I'd sound the same if I tried to speak. Assuming I could even form words at this juncture in the evening. "I can't believe I'm here with you."

I was having trouble believing it, too. I'd thought about this, but of course not admitted it to myself and the reality was far better than the fantasy. Since I wasn't sure I could talk I decided to let my fingers do the walking and show him that I was glad we were both in my bedroom.

Taking a few steps forward, I slid my hands under his sweater to the warm smooth skin underneath before beginning to tug it upward, leaving no doubt that I wanted it gone from his person. He quickly received my message and stripped it off, exposing the most beautiful man-chest I'd ever seen. Not too muscular but not too thin. I felt a little like Goldilocks.

Kyle was just right.

Now he was on a roll. His jeans were efficiently dispatched to the chair next to my bed, his socks following. He was a boxer-type guy, but I could see the hard ridge of his cock clearly outlined against the plaid cotton. With my palm I rubbed against it and drew a moan from his lips. His hips canted forward as his hands reached for me, pulling me closer, and his fingers dove into my hair as his mouth devoured mine, more dominant than before.

I hooked my thumbs in the waistband of his boxers and pushed them down over his perfectly formed backside. They slid down his thighs and to the floor where we both promptly ignored them. My gaze was fixed on the bounty that I had uncovered. Dropping to my knees, I wrapped my hands around his cock, enjoying the feeling of velvety skin with solid steel underneath. I leaned forward and took a swipe at the purplish-red head with my tongue, smiling with triumph when I heard a hiss and a groan from above me. His fingers tightened in my hair, silently urging me on but not being pushy about it. Once again, he'd left it up to me to take that next step.

I took a giant leap, opening my jaws and taking him in as far as I possibly could. He bumped the back of my throat and that's when I began a slow and steady rhythm with my lips and tongue that I hoped would drive him crazy. I'd never been a connoisseur of male anatomy but in my humble opinion Kyle's was beautiful. Long and thick, with blue-purple veins that created a meandering road map from crown to root. The tip of my tongue traced that path before swirling around the head again and again until he was panting and groaning, his grip on my hair almost painful.

"Baby, if you keep that up this is going to be over pretty quick and I have a few things I want to do to you, too."

Pulling off with a pop, I looked up at Kyle. "Such as?"

He frowned and shook his head. "I don't understand."

"You said there were things you wanted to do to me. Such as?"

With a chuckle, a grin spread across his terribly handsome face. "To begin with I want to get the rest of your clothes off of you."

"And then?"

Okay, I admit it. I kind of liked dirty talk. I just wasn't ready to tell him out loud. I was hoping he'd get the hint.

"I was planning to give your nipples and breasts some attention."

I tapped my chin and nodded as if considering his offer, but my heart was galloping as if I was being chased by demons. "That sounds good. Anything else?"

His answer was to reach down and lift me up off of the floor, tossing me gently onto the bed. He came down on top of me, caging me in with his arms. I liked it. A whole lot. "I have a couple more things in mind. My mouth between your thighs and then my cock. Does that meet your approval?"

Heavens yes. It sounded perfect.

"I wouldn't object."

"You wouldn't, huh?" Bending his head, he captured my bra strap in between his teeth and tugged playfully. "Then let's get you naked. Clothes will only slow me down."

Not much, though. Quickly and efficiently he stripped me, tossing my undergarments over his shoulder and onto the floor. Immediately he zeroed in on my already hard nipples, plucking at one with a free hand while he laved the other with his incredibly talented tongue. Shuddering with pleasure, I closed my eyes and let him take the reins.

I couldn't help but wonder what else that tongue could do.

I didn't have to wonder too long. He placed damp kisses down my abdomen, pushing my thighs apart to make room for his wide shoulders. My fingers wound in the bedsheets as his tongue ran through my folds, making me moan and arch with his skill. I should have known he'd be good at this. He was good at pretty much everything and he made it a point to practice at those things he thought he needed to improve. I had to admire his dedication.

Kyle could practice on me anytime.

When his mouth finally closed over my swollen clit I went up in flames, happily surrendering to the heat that engulfed me head to toe. I might have called out his name as I orgasmed harder than I ever had in my life, but I couldn't say for sure. All I knew was the room was spinning and the bed felt like I was bobbing on the ocean. For all I knew I could be. At that moment, anything was possible.

Sliding up so we were face to face, nose to nose, he rubbed his body against mine. My skin was so sensitive I trembled in his arms before pressing a kiss to his shoulder and then his neck. His flesh tasted salty and I licked at it, tickling his collar bone.

"Just give me one minute."

Kyle leaned over the edge of the bed and rummaged in the pockets of his jeans before coming back, a triumphant smile on his lips. He was holding up a small foil square. Thank goodness one of us was thinking clearly. With a minimum of fuss, he'd rolled it on with some help from me.

Reaching down, I placed my hands on his firm buttocks, urging him forward. He pressed into me, his hard cock almost splitting me in two. It had been a long time between lovers and it took me a moment to get used to his invasion. Taking a few deep breaths, he paused, his face a controlled mask as my body grew accustomed to being so fully impaled.

Stretched. That was the word I was looking for. I wrapped my legs around his hips and clutched his shoulders, wordlessly letting him know that I wanted him to move. When he finally did, the first few strokes took my breath away and then by the third or fourth it was as if we'd been doing this together forever.

Our bodies found a pleasurable rhythm, slow in the beginning and then moving faster and harder as we neared our crescendo. The half-lit room was filled with the sounds of our lovemaking. Short, desperate pants and groans. Damp skin slapping together. The headboard banging against the wall and the insistent creak of a bedspring. The heady aroma of sex hanging in the humid air. The tang of salt when his lips captured mine. It was erotic and hot and it didn't take long until I was once more teetering on the edge.

My nails dug into his back and I rocked my pelvis against his, getting the perfect friction that I needed. Recognizing my desired angle, he shifted slightly and hit that sweet spot inside of me over and over again while rubbing my clit on the outside. I couldn't hold back with the combined magic, it was all too much.

I exploded, warm liquid pleasure suffusing every millimeter of my body all the way to the tips of my toes and fingers. Letting it wash over me, I watched fascinated as Kyle reached his own peak, his head thrown back and his teeth bared in a growl of male satisfaction. When it was over he rolled to his back, taking me with him and tucking me into his side. Neither of us spoke for several minutes, too busy trying to suck oxygen into our starved lungs.

I didn't want to be the first to talk and break the spell. It felt so comfortable and cozy, just Kyle and I in our own little bubble. Reality was overrated.

So of course, I was the first one to say something. Because I simply couldn't shut up. Not even at a moment like this.

"That was…wow. Just wow."

Holy crap, I should have stayed quiet. So eloquent. Not. He probably thought he'd fucked my brains out.

"Can't disagree." Kyle sighed and pulled me closer so my head was pillowed on his chest. "You pack a wallop for such a little thing."

"Is that good?"

Did I say that out loud? I really needed to shut the hell up.

I could feel his chest rumble under my ear. "Very good. Very, very good. So good, in fact, that I'm going to want to do this again as often as possible. I hope that's not a problem."

It wasn't.

"Eventually we're going to have to go to work."

"True, but that's hours away."

I couldn't think of a better way to spend the time between now and then.

CHAPTER FOURTEEN

Ashlyn

DANCING CAN LEAD to making love. Making love all night can lead to falling asleep, exhausted and dead to the world. That means waking up the next morning with a new lover, a state I tried to avoid as much as possible.

I usually start laying the groundwork early in the date if I think there's a chance that we'll have sex. I tell him about how I have to get up for work or maybe catch a plane for a business trip. Later in the evening I'll make sure to touch on the subject again, just in case he wasn't listening the first time. If he's interested in the topic, I'll regale him with all the details of just how busy I'm going to be the next day and how tired I'll be at the end of it.

For some reason I had never been comfortable with waking up next to someone, most especially that first morning after. Some men were playful and wanted to continue the intimacy with a shared shower or more fooling around in the bed. Some men weren't morning people and needed an immediate cup of coffee. Which I completely understood. Some men couldn't get out of a woman's house fast enough, barely taking time to say good morning before they were in their car and driving down the road.

But they were all going to see my morning hair and smooshed bed face. They were going to be assaulted by my morning coyote breath.

And most of all…they were going to see my naked body in the cold, bright light of day. People always look better in candlelight and when Mister Sunshine rolls out of bed and beams into my bedroom window both me and the guy are going to get an eyeful that we may not have wanted.

So here I am lying in my own bed, the sun peeking through the curtains and casting a sunbeam across the comforter.

And I'm all alone.

Kyle was across town in his own home, probably curled up with Sam. I hadn't had to make any excuses this time. He'd had the excuse. He wanted to stay snuggled against me but he couldn't leave Sam alone all night. It made complete sense and I'd immediately agreed that he needed to get home to his puppy, but then after he'd left the bed hadn't been quite as comfortable and definitely not as warm and cozy.

Scratch that. Make that sizzling. Kyle Lewis really was a freakin' genius.

Searingly hot images crowded my brain as last night came screeching back. Kyle had been as thorough as I'd thought he'd be. Considerate but passionate. Rough but gentle. Insatiable but satisfying. And for some crazy reason I hadn't wanted him to leave last night. I'd wanted him to stay and wake up next to him. It had sounded so romantic in my head.

I needed coffee. A shower and coffee, not necessarily in that order. Maybe a cruller, too.

I might also need a trip to see Shelby at her office because I should have my head examined by a professional. I was already missing Kyle and wondering when I was going to see him again.

I was in deep with this guy. Heaven help me.

★　★　★

Kyle

I'D BARELY SLEPT last night after I arrived back home. Sam had jumped all over me and then went straight to the back door, indicating that he'd had his paws crossed waiting for me. I let him out and then we'd climbed into bed, but my head was too full of Ashlyn. How could I sleep after making love to the most beautiful woman in the world?

Next time we'd have to come back to my place so she could spend the night. I wanted to wake up with her in my arms, the warmth and scent of her skin surrounding me. I wanted to make love to her again, softly and slowly in the bright morning sunshine. As gorgeous as she'd looked last night, she'd be even more devastating with the sun glinting off her golden hair and caressing her peaches and cream complexion.

I wanted to spend the whole day with her too, but we both had work. There was that annoying little voice in the back of my head that was telling me that I was the boss and I could just call George and say I was taking the day off. But I didn't get where I am calling in sick on a whim. I doubted that Ashlyn did, either.

Damn, sometimes it sucked being a responsible adult.

After feeding Sam, I sat down on my couch with a cup of coffee and propped my feet on the coffee table while some newscaster droned on and on about world affairs and the weather. It was going to be another cold and snowy day in the Midwest. All I could think about was Ashlyn and I keeping warm. I could fix dinner for her tonight and then we could make love in front of the fireplace.

Except I hadn't made any future plans with Miss Hill before I left her house. Shit. I was dumb as a box of rocks about interpersonal relationships but even I knew that a gentleman needed to make a date as soon as possible after having sex. I didn't want Ashlyn to think that last night was…one night only.

Retrieving my phone from the side table, I tapped out a quick message. I didn't know if she woke early or slept late but at least she wouldn't think I'd flaked out on her.

Thinking about you.

Last night was fantastic.

How about dinner tonight? My place. I'll cook.

Should I have mentioned last night? Was it gauche or bad manners? It was the truth. I was thinking about her and last night was terrific. I wasn't the kind of guy to play games with a woman and I didn't want to pretend.

I didn't expect a reply so quickly but my phone buzzed almost instantaneously.

That sounds good. I'll bring the wine and dessert.

Okay…

Was that it? Was that all she was going to say? A cold sweat broke over me at the thought that perhaps last night hadn't been as good for Ashlyn as it had been for me, but then I remembered the way she'd said my name over and over, digging her nails into my back. This morning I'd had little crescent moons on my shoulders. So she'd enjoyed herself. Unless she was the most amazing actress ever.

Mentally smacking myself in the head, I pushed all the doubts from my mind. A guy had to have confidence or the world would trounce all over him. That's what I needed right now. Confidence and plenty of it. Because if I hadn't rocked Ashlyn's world...

Then I was determined to get a second chance tonight.

★ ★ ★

Ashlyn

EMMY HAD STOPPED into the store first thing to hear all about the date and had ended up sitting on a stool by the sales counter, paging through Shelby's book and sipping the coffee she'd brought us. And two cinnamon Danish. It was even better than a cruller. Hallelujah.

She tapped at the pages of the book. "I hate to admit it but the farther I read into this, the better it gets. The first part reads a trifle old-fashioned but after about the first third it really becomes a rallying cry for female empowerment. Shelby tells it like it is and she certainly tells her readers not to take any shit. I love it."

"I need to finish it," I admitted, stuffing another bite of warm cinnamon goodness in my mouth and savoring the sweet frosting, which was really the best part. The store was empty of customers and Katie was out running an errand so there was only my friend to witness my gluttony. "But I don't know when I'll be able to. Kyle asked me out again for tonight."

Wagging her brows, Emmy grinned. "That's what I'm here for. All the dirty details and don't be stingy. How was last night?"

There was no point in pretending with my best friend. She could see right through me and vice versa.

"It was really great." I paused, unsure how to phrase it. "I invited him in after the movie."

"Is that a euphemism for hitting the sheets? Having sex? Doing the dance with no pants?"

I giggled at her ridiculous sayings. "Where in the hell did you ever hear doing the *dance with no pants?*"

She rolled her eyes and groaned. "A best man said it at the toast a few weekends ago at a wedding I was organizing. He thought it was hilarious."

"He said it at the toast? How...cringeworthy. Somehow I don't think he was the *best man*, if you know what I mean."

"I worry for that relationship. The bride was not amused but her groom and his friends laughed and laughed. The stories I could tell you would curl your hair. I swear that woman married a thirteen-year-old in a grown man's body. Good luck to her because she's going to need it. Now enough about my weddings and get to it, missy. What happened?"

"We danced for a little while and then we ended up in bed."

Emmy was literally rubbing her hands together like a villain in a bad movie.

"Excellent. He's a smooth fucker, I'll give him that. Or wait... Did he suggest dancing or did you?"

"He did. I was so nervous I think he thought it would relax me." I sighed and took another bite of my cinnamon Danish.

"He relaxed me all the way to making love and it made it like it was my idea. I was the one that suggested we take it to the bedroom."

Emmy's eyes widened and her mouth fell open. "He's got skill. So…does he have real skill? The kind that counts?"

The truth will set you free.

"Yes. Oh my, yes. It was amazing. Earthshattering. Life changing."

"Wow, that's some incredible sex."

"It was."

"You could seem happier about it."

"I am happy. It's just that I feel like I'm riding a runaway train and I don't know how much track is there. This could derail badly."

"Or it could be really wonderful. What are you afraid of?"

Did she want the list alphabetical or by importance?

"How can you even ask that? You know who he is and you know who I am. I can't change for him and I won't."

"Has he asked you to change?"

The cinnamon roll was gone so all I had left was my coffee. Mental note. Keep more snacks in the storeroom.

"No, but they don't do it at the beginning. You know that. They wait until you've fallen for them and that's when they start to try and change you. A little at first, and then more. Like that boiling the frog story." I held up my phone and waved it around. I was still indignant about it an hour later. "Do you know how he asked me out for tonight? By text. Text, Emmy. He said last night was great and how about dinner tonight. He'll cook. It was a *text.*"

Patting my hand, Emmy gave me a kind look. "I know you hate cell phone communication of any kind but that is a perfectly acceptable way to ask a person out on a date these days."

I stared down at my phone with distaste. The only reason I had a smart phone like this was because Emmy had taken me – practically by force – to the cell phone store and forced me to upgrade from my flip phone. My friends wanted to be able to send me texts and pictures and whatever else. There was nothing wrong with my flip phone. It got the job done but I had to admit that sending a text wasn't easy and it took forever for one little sentence.

But I still didn't like it.

"I slept with a man who thinks it's okay to ask out a woman by text. What have I done? We're just too different."

Emmy took the last drink of her coffee and then tossed the cup into the trash. "Here's a radical thought. Why don't you tell him you don't like to text? I'm sure he'll understand."

"It might be too early in our relationship for that sort of honesty."

"But it's not too early to do naked, sweaty things with him on your Egyptian cotton sheets? Really?"

Emmy was the most practical of the four of us and today was no exception. Dammit. But then she hadn't been there last night as Kyle and I had danced. The heat, the tension, the shimmering attraction that couldn't be ignored.

Was it hot in here? I think I turned the heat up too far when I opened the store.

"You make a good point. I'll bring it up with him tonight. If he doesn't take it well, then I guess I'll know that this won't work."

"Stop looking for reasons to end this," Emmy chided me. "Look for ways to make it work. What are your deal-breakers?"

I had no idea, but I know that Mia had made a list of what she wanted and didn't want when she was working through Shelby's book.

Sighing, I reached for a notebook under the counter and a pen rolling around by the register.

"I don't know but I'll make a list. Are you going to help me?"

"Absolutely." She clapped her hands together and then paged to that part of the book. "Now tell me what kind of man you can see yourself with when you're eighty."

"The kind that pick my ass up off the floor when I fall."

I might enjoy this exercise after all.

"Funny. Seriously, what's the most important trait a man can have?"

"A sense of humor. That's an easy one. How many more questions are there?"

"Seventy-four."

"I think we're going to need more coffee."

CHAPTER FIFTEEN

Kyle

I F IT HADN'T been snowing and the temperature a frosty twenty-five degrees Fahrenheit, I would have done steaks on the grill. With the weather the way it was, however, I needed a plan B.

My mother had taught all of us kids to cook a few basic dishes – grilled cheese, spaghetti and meatballs, and her famous chicken. The chicken involved a hell of a lot of garlic but it always made the house smell heavenly. Since I wanted to impress Ashlyn with my culinary skills, I picked up a roaster and some potatoes and carrots from the store along with a half-gallon of ice cream, hot fudge, and whipped cream. She'd indicated that she was bringing dessert but just in case I wanted to be prepared.

My dirty mind had already thought of a few scenarios of where we could put that hot fudge and whipped cream to use if we didn't eat the ice cream.

I'd straightened up the house, lit a fire in the fireplace, and put fresh sheets on the bed. Just in case.

Okay, I'm a total horndog.

Freshly showered and dressed, I had just checked on the chicken and potatoes in the oven when I heard the peal of the doorbell. My pulse raced with excitement and I opened the door to see Ashlyn on the other side looking more beautiful than I'd remembered. She was dressed casually in blue jeans and a sweater under her thick coat but she'd left her long blonde hair down around her shoulders. I couldn't resist rubbing a silky strand between my fingers as I kissed her hello.

The air around us quickly heated up, and I had to drag my mouth from hers to slow my arousal and keep from jerking her up into my arms and dragging her to bed. Sam, too, was being particularly insistent that she pay some attention to him and not me. It seemed that I had a rival for her affections and he was damn cuter than me. How could I possibly compete?

I'd pulled her in for a kiss so quickly I hadn't even said hello or noticed that she was carrying a bottle of wine and an oblong pan.

"Will you take these so I can give our sweet boy a big hug and kiss?" I relieved her of her burdens and she practically dove onto the floor to press her cheek against Sam's fur. "Hello, love. How are you? Are you getting spoiled?"

The dog was getting more attention for sure.

"He got a bath today," I said, ruffling the shining fur on his back. "He really needed it. I thought he'd hate it, but he loved it. Didn't want to get out of the tub."

"I'll get you a rubber duckie," she cooed, kissing Sam on his snout. "Don't you look handsome? And you smell so good."

"Hey, I smell good, too," I said in mock indignation. Mostly mock. "I bathed as well. No rubber duckie required."

Once again, my filthy mind filled with images of me and Ashlyn in my oversized jetted bathtub. A tub that Sam *had not* been bathed in this afternoon. I'd used the guest bathroom for that.

She abandoned Sam and lifted up on her tiptoes to give me a chaste kiss on the cheek. Probably just as well or we'd end up with a burnt dinner. "Are you feeling left out? He's just so cute and look at him wag his tail. He really earned it."

Sam was really going all out to win Ashlyn's affections. His tail was wagging, his tongue hanging out, and he was looking up at her with pure love in his brown gaze. A human guy simply couldn't compete with that.

"I was glad to see you too, and I would have happily run around like that if I thought I was going to get all of that affection. Come on, Sam. Let's escort our guest into the kitchen and pour her a glass of wine. It's never too early to learn to be a good host."

"That would have been a sight to see. Kyle Lewis prancing around like a puppy."

Uncorking the wine, I smirked at her suggestion. "Worse things have been said about me."

Her smile dimmed and her expression turned into a frown. "How do you deal with all of that?"

"I don't." I handed her a half-full glass. "I don't read what people write about me. Most of the time. Everyone has an opinion. If I let all the negative press get to me, I'd never do anything. I just keep my head down and focus on the work. I have a public relations firm that handles the rest."

"Are they handling people like me?"

Astute question. I should have anticipated that Ashlyn would ask it, but I had no problem answering it honestly.

"Yes, to a certain extent. There is a small percentage of the population that is sure that I'm going to bring on the robot uprising and the fall of humanity."

"The fall of humanity? On one man's shoulders? That seems unlikely. There are others out there doing what you're doing."

"They're not thinking with logic. This is all about emotion. Don't get the two confused."

Something flitted across her face, quick but it was there.

"Do you think I'm doing this out of emotion?"

"A little bit. Yes."

Guess who might be eating dinner all alone tonight? Me. But I couldn't lie.

"A little bit," she repeated. "That sounds like a cop-out to me."

"I think it's the truth." I took a gulp of wine that I desperately needed. I was hoping for romance but this had taken a turn. "There's emotion behind your plea to save those houses because you love and respect the past. Those are emotions, Ashlyn. If you were making decisions based on logic you would have advocated for those houses to be bulldozed years ago and put in a parking lot. I'm kind of hoping that we can have some sort of compromise."

It was the first I'd mentioned it because I didn't know if it would even work, but I didn't want her to think that I was some mindless robot raping the land for fun and profit.

Her eyes widened in surprise. "Compromise? You think that there's a compromise?"

Another gulp of my wine. "I didn't want to mention it until I knew something for certain – which I don't yet – but I am trying to see if any of those houses are salvageable. If so, I was thinking that maybe I could save one or two and turn them into residences for visiting academics."

I should have braced myself because Ashlyn launched herself into my arms, almost knocking the wine out of my glass and onto the floor. Pressing kisses all over my face, I suddenly knew how Sam felt.

Pretty damn fine. Lucky dog.

"Wait," I cautioned, placing my glass on the kitchen counter. "Hold on a minute. I said I was looking into it. I don't know if it's even possible. Ashlyn, those houses are in terrible shape. A real hazard. There may not be any saving them."

I didn't want her to get her hopes too high and then have them come crashing down to earth when reality set in. I was trying to save a house or two, but the odds were against me.

"But you're trying," she said, pressing another kiss to the corner of my mouth. I wanted to take these accolades but I hadn't earned them yet. "You're really trying and that means the world to me."

"George is talking to a structural engineering firm about it. They'll be the final decision makers," I warned. "If they say no, then it won't happen. Can you live with that?"

She'd calmed down slightly but her color was still high with excitement. I shouldn't have opened my big fat mouth, but I wanted to make her feel better. And yes, I wanted her approval.

"I can. I just means so much to me that you're even exploring this."

"You made a good case at the city council meeting."

"I did, didn't I?" With a wide smile, she sniffed the air. "Is that chicken and...garlic? It smells delicious."

"It is. How about you relax with your wine and I'll set the table? It should be ready in a few minutes."

"I wouldn't say no. Is there anything I can do to help, though?"

"Everything is under control." Except my libido. "Seriously, just put your feet up and relax. I've got this."

"A handsome man and dinner. What more could I ask for?"

This woman could ask me for anything and I'd move heaven and earth to get it for her.

I'd fallen that fast and that hard.

★ ★ ★

Ashlyn

DINNER WAS DELICIOUS. When I'd praised Kyle for his culinary prowess he'd laughed and told me that he had an extremely limited repertoire. The garlic chicken was his mother's recipe and he was more than happy to share it with me.

There was something about a man cooking for me that had me all aflutter. I'd spent most of dinner with flushed cheeks as my mind went to places it had no business being.

At least this early in the evening.

Kyle was the whole package. Handsome, intelligent, funny, sensitive, caring, and a great lover. I'd been thinking about last night all day, and any doubts that I'd then were pushed away by just how wonderful this was between us. I was happy. Really happy. There had been fear this morning, but it didn't stand a chance against this man in full romance mode.

By the end of the meal, I was full and had imbibed two glasses of wine leaving me a content and a little sleepy. I hadn't brought up the whole *text thing* because I hadn't wanted to ruin the comfortable vibe we had going tonight. Plus, I was beginning to wonder if I was making a big deal out of nothing. This was the twenty-first century and texting was a major mode of communication. Just because it bothered me didn't mean that he'd been rude or had to stop doing it. Maybe I needed to change.

Standing from the kitchen island, Kyle picked up our empty plates and carried them to the sink. Sam was right on his heels hoping for a handout but he wasn't going to get one. He had been given some plain chicken earlier, but Sam was adamant about not giving him the spiced version.

"Give me five minutes to pop these in the dishwasher and then I'll turn on a movie. Anything you want to watch. It's your choice."

"Can I help?"

There wasn't much as he'd cleaned up as he'd cooked but I wanted to be a good guest.

"I've got it. Why don't you pick out a movie?"

He had an impressive collection of DVDs on his bookshelf in the living room, so Sam and I looked through the titles.

I looked. Sam sniffed.

I chose *The Maltese Falcon* and the canine seemed to approve, giving it a good sniff and wagging his tail. Turning on Kyle's television, I popped the movie into the player and sat down on the sofa. There was a stack of drawings on the coffee table and I was immediately sucked in, studying them closely and generally being nosy.

"Those are proposals for the technical campus."

I looked up to see Kyle holding out another glass of wine, which I accepted with a mental note to just sip it. Three glassed was my absolute limit.

He settled in next to me and pointed to one of the drawings. "That's my favorite so far."

I had to admit it wasn't the glass and metal monstrosity I'd envisioned. Several brick buildings all facing a lush green courtyard were the main focus of the design. The courtyard boasted a sculpture garden but didn't specify what sort of art might be displayed there.

"It's nice. But none of these have the houses in them."

A small measure of doubt was creeping into my psyche. Could Kyle simply be paying lip service to my cause? I didn't want to think so...

"Because I'm not sure we can save the houses. Once the structural engineers say we can, I can go back to the competing architects and ask them to include that in their proposals."

"None of these designs would preserve the architecture of those homes."

"That's true. But on the bright side, none of them are modern eyesores, either. Wasn't that your biggest fear? That the campus would stand out and not mesh into the environment? The architects have worked hard to make sure that doesn't happen."

They had and a few of the drawings were quite impressive. Kyle was going all out for his dream and it showed.

I shrugged, not sure how to express all the feelings running riot inside of me. Hope. Fear. And a few more I couldn't even identify.

"Some of these are amazing. I guess I'm just hoping that you get good news from the engineers." I took a deep breath. "And I hope that some of the architectural details from the homes can be saved."

Kyle tugged the drawings from my fingers and placed them on the coffee table before wrapping an arm around me and pulling me close. "I'm going to do my very best, Ashlyn, but I need to know that you're going to be okay if I fail."

There was real fear in his voice and I had put it there. Not my proudest moment. This was a new relationship though, and we had much to learn about each other.

"I will be. I'm just glad that you tried."

"And you'll be okay if the engineers say it can't be done?"

There was a part of me that wanted to ask about a second or third opinion but then I reminded myself that Kyle wouldn't employ anyone but the best.

"Yes, but I might be sad about it."

"Then I'll do my best to cheer you up."

Time to lighten up the conversation.

"With sex? Because that doesn't solve every single problem in the world."

"It doesn't?" He looked at me with mock horror and I couldn't stop giggling as he placed his hand over his heart and sighed dramatically. "This is such awful news. Sex can't solve every problem? Are you sure? Because I've been told differently."

"Who? By your friends?" I teased, sliding a hand up his muscular thigh and feeling him tense under my fingers. "It can solve one problem we have."

His palm cupped my cheek, sending a tingle through my body and straight to parts in the southerly direction. "What problem is that, beautiful?"

Warmth rushed through my veins at his endearment. I took most compliments with a grain of salt, but he sounded sincere. "The problem of how we could build up an appetite for dessert."

His smile was heartbreakingly gorgeous and my own stomach fluttered in response.

"I have a few ideas. If you're game?"

"You are the genius."

Dessert could wait. I couldn't.

CHAPTER SIXTEEN

Ashlyn

"I MIGHT BE in love."

I made my announcement to Shelby and Emmy at brunch the next Sunday. I didn't have to go work at the shelter today because Natalie was training a few new volunteers. I might drop in one afternoon during the week though, just to walk a few dogs. But that meant I had the whole day to myself.

I'd met my friends at our usual restaurant and I was planning on ordering everything on the menu. I was starving. My appetite was working overtime this last week.

Kyle was on a business trip to San Francisco which meant I had been able to get a full night's sleep. Despite the fact that we'd spent most of the last ten nights making love, I didn't appear sleep-deprived in the least. It was kind of a miracle. I was getting maybe four hours a night – five or six if I was lucky – and I didn't have the usual hollow-eyed, pasty skin look at all.

I was glowing. My eyes sparkled, my skin was flushed with color, and I was wearing a goofy smile most of the time. Even my regular customers had noticed and remarked that I seemed in a terrific mood. Katie would hear them comment and almost spit out her coffee laughing, but I just thanked them and smiled.

"You're not in love. You're getting laid," Emmy replied bluntly. "Don't get sex all confused with love. It's too soon to be in love."

"It's not too soon," Shelby argued. "You can know the first time you meet them."

"I don't believe in love at first sight," I replied while scanning the menu. The waffles looked good but so did the eggs Benedict. And some bacon. Maybe a Danish or two. "But I'm definitely not acting like myself. I think about him all the time. It's crazy."

Shelby nodded in understanding. "We know. We've barely seen you in the last week and a half."

"You've missed yoga three times in a row," Emmy said. "The instructor even asked me about you, thinking you might be sick or injured."

"Now you're just trying to make me feel guilty. It's just a yoga class, and that instructor is always dramatic. If I tell him that I have a cold, he thinks I have typhoid."

He was a germaphobe and if anyone so much as sneezed he practically threw them out of class.

I ended up ordering the waffles with a side of everything. Plus a Mimosa.

"What do you two do every night?" Emmy asked as the waitress disappeared into the kitchen. "And please spare me any graphic details. I haven't had a full cup of coffee yet."

Kyle and I were having a great deal of sex, but it wasn't all that we were doing.

"We have dinner. I cook or he cooks or we go out," I explained. "We watch television or we work. We walk Sam and play with him. Thursday night I helped Kyle give Sam a bath."

"Very domestic," Shelby observed. "You're settling right in. Of course, you know what the book says about that."

Actually, I didn't. I'd been so busy I hadn't finished it yet.

Yes, I felt guilty about it.

"Of course, I do."

Shelby and Emmy exchanged a glance and then the former gave me a mean-eyed look. "No, you don't. You haven't read it all yet. Admit it."

My friends were beginning to piss me off. Shelby was supposed to be a psychologist, not a mind reader.

"Fine, I haven't finished it yet. I've been really busy. But I think I get where you're going with all of this. You know...the gist of it all."

That's it...the gist.

Shelby sighed as the waitress placed our drinks on the table. "It's important to read it all. If you had, you would know that I don't advise all this cozy domesticity until he's committed to an exclusive relationship. Has he?"

"Is this about cows and free milk?" I asked suspiciously. "Because that's just sexist. My grandmother would have a stroke if she saw just the title of your book."

As my close friends, Emmy and Shelby – and Mia too – knew all about my famous grandmother.

"This is not about cows, free milk, or your grandmother," Shelby said. "This is about making sure that you're getting as much as you're giving in a relationship. It's also about not allowing him to start nesting with you while he's still out dating around. If he wants Netflix and chill, he better keep it at home.

If you know what I mean."

I knew what she meant and she had a point. But it didn't apply here.

"Kyle hasn't had time to see anyone else. He's with me every night."

"Every single night?" Emmy asked, her brows raised in question. "You've spent every single night with Kyle in the last ten days?"

"Okay, not every single night," I conceded. "But almost every night. We're together. A couple."

Shelby took a sip of her Bloody Mary. "Did he specifically say that you two were an exclusive couple?"

"No, but he didn't have to." Their expression said it all. "I don't have to explain myself here. I just know. A woman knows when a man is still looking. Kyle is not looking, okay?"

Emmy raised her hands in surrender. "It's not us you have to convince. This is just Shelby's advice. You can take it or leave it."

"Mia took it and look what happened," Shelby pointed out, triumph in her tone. "She's happy and in love."

"I'm going to paraphrase Emmy for a moment." I held up one finger. "You have one success story. One. And Mia and Josh probably would have ended up together anyway."

"Maybe, but they weren't making any progress until I stepped in."

"Mia was in that store robbery," Emmy said. "That changed her, too."

"All we're saying is to be careful," Shelby said. "We love you and we want the best for you. If Kyle Lewis is it, then we're thrilled."

"I'm really happy."

"Then we're happy," Emmy assured me. "So it's time to take the next step."

I was genuinely fearful to ask what that might be. Kyle and I had only been dating for a week and a half. I wasn't ready to get engaged or to ask for a key to his house.

"The next step?"

Shelby spread her arms wide and grinned. "To meet us, of course. When can we do it?"

How did two weeks from never sound?

★ ★ ★

EMMY AND I ended up at our favorite clothing store after breakfast. She didn't get too many weekends off, but the dead of winter was a slow time for weddings. She was about to ramp up in a big way as Valentine's Day approached, though. Since she had the afternoon free, we decided to do a little damage to our credit cards.

I was in the changing room and Emmy was handing me clothes over the top of the door for me to try on. She had better fashion taste than I did, and I wanted a few new outfits to dazzle Kyle.

"So what is your deal?" I heard her ask through the flimsy slats of the door. Passersby could only see the bottom of my legs, thank goodness.

I pulled a gray sweater – that I had chosen – over my head and made a face. It sucked all the color from my skin. Note to self. Don't wear gray.

"My deal? I don't know what you mean."

"I mean why are you reluctant to bring your Prince Charming to meet us? It was obvious at breakfast that you hated the idea. We won't scare him off. We're nice people."

"Shelby will try to analyze him."

Emmy handed me a floaty pink blouse. Pink? Really? Sighing, I pulled it on and stood in awe. She really was amazing. It actually looked good.

"So? Shelby analyzes everyone. It's her thing. That's not a reason to keep him under wraps. What's going on?"

I stuck my head out of the dressing room. "I really like Kyle."

"You said that."

"I don't want to mess this up."

"That's half a sentence. What's the rest of it?"

Emmy knew me better than anyone.

"What if you meet Kyle and you love him but then the relationship doesn't work out?"

"Do you think we'll blame you? It takes two to tango. What is this really about, Ash?"

This time Emmy stepped into the dressing room with me as a few people were beginning to take note of our discussion and listening in. The one time people weren't looking at their phones...

"What's going on?" she asked again, but this time her voice was hushed. "I've never seen you like this. You've really fallen for him."

I had and it scared me to death.

"We're so different," I finally replied. "How can this work?"

"Because you want it to?"

"That's not enough."

"Can I just say that your grandmother has really done a number on you? She's so militant about those that don't believe what she believes. That cuts out half of the population. That's a lot of people, Ash. If you want something bad enough, you work for it." Emmy leaned back against the full-length mirror. "Isn't that what you've always said? You and Kyle might hit more rough patches but if it's good it will be worth it. My feeling, though, is that you've already decided that it's not going to work and are just waiting for it all to fall apart."

"It's almost too wonderful. When is reality going to smack us in the face?"

"It will when you least expect it but enjoy the wonder of new love while you can. It doesn't last forever."

"It didn't for my grandmother."

Emmy's brows shot up. "What do you mean?"

"She and my grandfather are divorced."

"I take it they had a nasty breakup?"

I nodded. "Gran always said that my grandpa was too different from her. That they didn't agree on anything. By the time I came to live with her, they'd just divorced. He remarried about a year later."

I'd seen him less and less after that until I stopped seeing him altogether. Gran hadn't encouraged it and he'd been busy with his new family.

"And that's why you're so freaked out about you and Kyle. You think history is going to repeat itself."

"Yes, I'm so much like my grandmother."

"But you are not her," Emmy said. "She made her decision and you are free to make your own. Listen, do you like Kyle?"

I did. So very much.

"I do."

"Do you think you could fall in love with him?"

Easily.

"Yes."

"Does he have some terrible habits? Does he smoke and blow it in your face? Does he flirt with waitresses and ignore you all evening? Does he run up wild tabs at expensive restaurants and expect you to pay the bill? These are all things that have happened to me, by the way."

"He would never do any of that to me."

Emmy rolled her eyes and sighed. "Then for the love of all that's good and holy, give yourself – and him – a break. Just relax and enjoy yourself. This might work out and it might not, but if it doesn't it may not be because he's a tech guy and you hate cell phones. It might be for far different reasons that you can't even fathom right now until you get to know each other better. He might cut his toenails in the kitchen. That would be a deal breaker for me."

Giggling at the image my friend had conjured, I was feeling somewhat better. "That's disgusting."

"Damn right, it's disgusting. So don't assume that you know how you and your man are going to end. If you're lucky, all his bad habits won't be hygiene related."

"You always make so much sense. How do you do it?"

Emmy gave me a smug smile. "I'm notoriously practical,

almost annoyingly so. I consider it a gift. Now what do you think of that pink blouse?"

"I think it's perfect. You were right again."

I wanted to believe that Emmy was right about everything, and that Kyle and I were going to be fine.

Relax and enjoy it. I could do that.

★　★　★

GEORGE AND I were supposed to be going through the budget for the next fiscal year. It was a bright and cold Monday morning and he'd brought over coffee and donuts as usual. We'd spread all the paperwork out on the coffee table while Sam snoozed on his doggie bed by the fireplace. I should have been concentrating on work, but my mind was elsewhere.

Specifically? On Ashlyn, and even more specifically on the invitation I received.

George pointed to a line item on the page in front of me. "So I'm thinking that the marketing budget should be a thousand percent of revenue."

Wait...what?

"What did you say?"

"Were you actually listening?" George smirked. "Because you've been a million miles away all morning. I suggested that everyone get thirty percent raises and you agreed. I'm going to hold you to that. At least for me. What is going on in your head? It's a woman, isn't it? It's always a woman. Einstein wasn't distracted by women."

"Einstein was a horn dog. They say he slept with Marilyn Monroe."

"Mozart?"

"A party animal."

"Da Vinci?"

"It was the Renaissance, dude."

"Tesla?"

"A major germaphobe and obsessed with the number three. So...no. But let's not forget Picasso or Hemingway. They had a few distractions of the female variety."

"So what's your story?"

Did I want to talk about it? Why not? George wasn't married or in a long-term relationship, but he might have some insight into the situation.

"Things have been going great with Ashlyn."

I'd never felt this strongly for a woman in my life, but I wasn't about to admit that to George.

"Is that a problem?"

"Not in the least. I was simply setting the stage. Anyway, things have been terrific. She's an amazing woman." I leaned back on the sofa, resting my head on the stuffed cushion. "She's invited me to a board game night with her friends."

"I'll ask the same question. Is that a problem? I would think it would be a good thing. She likes you enough to introduce you to her friends. You've made it past the first hurdle. Good for you."

"I'm looking forward to meeting her friends," I assured him. "They sound like interesting people. But I kind of wonder...if maybe...this is some sort of test."

"Test?"

"You know, do I pass muster? Will they be evaluating me? What if they don't like me?"

George snorted and Sam raised his head from his pillow. "Everyone likes you. Especially females. You're all charm and smiles when you're supposed to be socially awkward and introverted. I bet Isaac Newton was socially awkward."

"I have no idea. You should Google that."

"Seriously, you're thinking too much about this. Stop analyzing it all. That's your problem, you know. You analyze everything to death."

"That is definitely not my problem."

"It is this time. Just go and have a good time. Aren't you the tiniest bit interested in her friends and what they're like?"

I was. It would give me more insight into Ashlyn. I was in that phase of falling in love where I wanted to know every single thing about her down to her shoe size and what color the flecks were around the iris of her eyes.

Gray and gold.

"We should get you a woman, George. You're alone too much. That's your problem."

He shook his head. "My problem is that my boss is a workaholic and I never get any time off. Women don't like that."

"You should ask for a raise."

"I already did. I'm getting thirty percent this year."

Shit. I really needed to focus when George was around.

CHAPTER SEVENTEEN

Ashlyn

N EVER PLAY TRIVIAL Pursuit with a genius. Words to live by.

Kyle trounced all of us. It wasn't even close. He knew the answer to every single stinkin' question and the answers to all of our questions as well. I had never felt so stupid in my entire life. I have no idea what we were thinking choosing this game. We were tired of Monopoly. We'd played Uno last month. And Mia and Josh had most of the really good games at her place but since she was in Scotland at the moment we had limited choices. If I'd thought ahead I would have stopped at Target, but clearly I hadn't thought this through.

It didn't take him long to kick our asses, either. He'd won just as the pizzas arrived. Good timing. We could drown our sorrows in melted cheese. I filled my plate with pizza and topped up my giant margarita. Shelby was playing bartender. She'd made 'em strong and yummy.

Kyle and I sat on the floor in the living room with our dinner plates on the coffee table. I took a huge bite and hummed in appreciation. It was delicious. I'd been looking forward to this all day long. All I'd had to eat all day was a bagel in the morning and a package of cheese crackers in the afternoon.

In fact, it might have been a mistake to drink tequila on an empty stomach. The room wasn't spinning or anything, but I was happy to be seated instead of standing. I need to eat pronto.

"I'm really sorry," Kyle said softly into my ear. He smelled so good tonight. As always. I was already thinking about dragging him back to his place and having my wicked way with him.

Emmy had urged me to enjoy myself.

"What are you sorry for?"

"For winning."

His gaze ran over my friends, who were also find a seat and settling down to eat. Shelby was there, of course, and Brad for once wasn't on the phone. He was acting all pouty while sitting on the recliner in the corner. He didn't like to lose. Emmy was there as well with her current boyfriend Mark, who was an art professor at the local university. He'd taken losing quite well, laughing it off. I was kind of hoping Emmy and Mark might become serious about one another. They appeared to be well-matched and he was an all-around nice guy.

"It's not your fault you're so smart. They know that. Don't worry about it. We should have played gin rummy or poker."

He shook his head. "Don't ever play poker with me."

"Why?"

"Just don't. Trust me on this."

Okay... I wasn't a huge fan of poker anyway, so it was no great loss.

"You and Mark seem to be getting along well."

"He's a good guy."

I took a sip of my margarita, loving the burn of the tequila and the tartness of the lime. Why didn't I drink these more often? There was a pleasant warmth in my abdomen and I was feeling especially serene and mellow. I leaned close to Kyle, tugging at his shirt sleeve.

"Can I tell you a secret?"

My lips were so close to his ear I could have reached out with my tongue and taken a swipe at it. I was sorely tempted and had to concentrate on all the reasons I shouldn't do it. There didn't seem to be too many. I took a deep breath of his scent and a shiver went up my spine. Did I mention how good he smelled?

"You can, but should you?"

I leaned even closer, my gaze landing on Brad who had – surprise, surprise – pulled out his phone. Kyle wouldn't do that. At least he never had when I was around.

"You are getting so lucky tonight."

His brows shot up almost to his hairline and a grin spread across his face. "I am? What did I do to deserve that? I want to know so I can keep doing it."

"Everyone likes you. I didn't know how this was going to go," I confessed, my tongue loosened by tequila. "But my friends wanted to meet you."

"Your friends are nice people, honey. I'm glad they like me because I like them." He leaned down and brushed his lips over mine. He tasted of garlic and beer. "Can I tell you a secret? I was nervous about meeting your friends. I thought this might be a test of some sort."

"You're good at tests," I snorted. "You would have aced it."

His expression sobered. "Was it? A test, I mean?"

"Maybe a little. I wanted them to like you, but if they didn't it wouldn't have changed my mind."

My gaze rested on Brad again. I'd never told another living soul – not even Emmy – but I didn't like him. I thought Shelby could do better.

His gaze followed mine and he nodded. "Ah, I see. You've never said anything?"

"Never in a million years," I replied fervently. "It's not for me to decide. If she's happy then I'm happy for her. I think that's how my friends feel, too."

"Are you happy, Ashlyn Hill?"

There was hope in those eyes. Silly man…couldn't he tell?

"More than I ever thought I could be. Now eat your pizza so I can make an excuse and get us out of here. You're getting lucky."

And so was I.

★　★　★

Kyle

WE HIT THE door of her house like we were storming the beaches at Normandy. All the way there Ashlyn had teased me, running her hands up my thigh until my cock had a permanent imprint from the zipper on my jeans. By the time the door swung shut behind us and she'd flipped the lock on the door, I was ready to explode.

I had to have her. Now.

Later, I'd spend all night lavishing every inch of her flesh with attention but at the moment my only goal was to get inside of her as soon as possible.

Despite the freezing temperatures of February I was boiling from the inside out. This sexy, sweet, maddening woman had made me crazier than I'd ever been and we were never going to make it to the bedroom. For a split second I pondered the possibilities of the couch or the kitchen counter, but Ashlyn had already made the decision for me. Backing up against the foyer wall, she grabbed the front of my shirt and jerked me toward her. She didn't have to pull hard because I was more than willing.

Hell, I pressed her against the wall until I could feel every inch of her against every aching hard inch of me. One hand slid up under her skirt to the satiny soft skin of her thigh while the other dived into her silky tresses, tangling in her golden curls so I could tilt her head up and further plunder those lips that never ceased to drive me absolutely wild. I was falling so hard and so fast for this tiny little female and for the first time in my life I didn't fight it, content to jump off the cliff and see where I landed.

Burying my face in the fragrant hollow of her neck, I nipped at the sensitive flesh and then ran my tongue over the love bites. Ashlyn trembled in my arms and I was shaking as well, my senses overcome with pure desire.

The temperature in the room had to have gone up at least twenty degrees and our skin was now damp with sweat. My questing fingers slipped under the edge of her panties and I almost roared with anticipation and triumph. Wet and hot, my finger plunged into her as my thumb strummed her clit. A gasp and then a moan escaped from her lips as she clawed at the zipper on my pants. She was as desperate as I was.

Reaching between us, I yanked my fly down and pushed my jeans low on my hips along with my jockey shorts. My cock sprang free and her hand immediately wrapped around it, drawing a tortured groan from my throat. My chest rose and fell rapidly as I sucked oxygen into my starved lungs. Ashlyn literally took my breath away. I'd always thought that saying was silly but here I was…

Her talented fingers danced up and down my shaft and I simply couldn't take it anymore. Reaching under her bottom with my left arm, I hiked her up and braced her against the wall as I pushed her skirt up as well. The crotch of her panties was no barrier and easily set aside. I thrust into her, her heat surrounding me snug and tight.

Ashlyn's head was thrown back, her eyes heavy-lidded. Her hair was a tangled mess, her skin shiny with sweat, and her lips swollen from the ferocity of our kisses.

I'd never seen a more beautiful woman. She was perfection and – right now – she was all mine.

Our coupling was fast and not romantic in the least. We grunted and groaned in an indelicate manner, Ashlyn's voice was hoarse as she urged me to fuck her harder. Her hands had burrowed under my sweater and her nails dug into the skin on my shoulders, the small pain no match for the immeasurable pleasure of being so deeply inside of her.

The pressure in my lower back had built to a painful level but I needed Ashlyn to go over first. Insinuating my fingers between our bodies I found her clit, swollen and ready. It only took a few flicks of my fingers and she was soaring into the stars with me following quickly after.

My toes curled and my teeth gritted together as my climax singed all of the nerve endings in my spine. I had to lock my knees to keep from falling into a boneless, mindless heap on the floor, but somehow I managed to keep both of us from spraining something vital. Our breathing was ragged and labored but we were both wearing goofy grins on our faces. I couldn't see mine, but I could feel it.

Euphoria. That's what it was. We were both high on endorphins. I wanted to do this six times a day for the rest of my damn life.

"Well…that escalated quickly," she whispered, her lips against the sensitive skin of my jaw. I pressed a chaste kiss to her forehead and then her lips, scraping her damp hair back from her cheek.

"It did. Want to do it again? Maybe in a more comfortable location?" I let her feet slide to the floor, but I kept a hold of her in case her legs gave out. "After proper rehydration, of course."

"Of course." She fiddled with the hem of my sweater, her fingertips brushing my skin and sending arrows of heat straight to my groin. It was like I was a horny teenager again. "Meet me in the bedroom?"

My answer would always be yes.

CHAPTER EIGHTEEN

Kyle

TWO WEEKS LATER, I slung my duffel over my shoulder and then reached for Ashlyn's backpack, but she lightly smacked my hand away. We were finally checking in at the resort after a long morning of travel.

"I can get that. It's not that heavy."

Paying no attention to her scolding, I picked up the backpack anyway. She was wrong. It was heavy and I had to wonder for a moment just what in the hell she'd packed in there. An anvil? Was I in Florida with Wile E. Coyote? How was she even lugging it around? It weighed more than she did.

I would know too, because I'd picked Ashlyn up and carried her to the bedroom more than once.

"I'm being a gentleman," I said, leading the way to the hotel elevator. The bellman would bring up the larger suitcases. "Some people would be really happy about that."

"I am happy. I'm also capable of carrying my own bag."

"I never said you weren't."

The elevator silently swept us upstairs to the suite I'd reserved, Ashlyn giving me a sour look the entire way. I'd found out a few things about my girlfriend on this trip and the most important one was that she wasn't the hardiest of travelers. First there had been a delay with our flight and she'd paced the first-class lounge like an expectant father while I drank my coffee and ate everything on the breakfast buffet. Then there had been a little turbulence over Atlanta and that had turned her a nasty shade of green. Then after we'd landed she'd paced the baggage area, certain that our luggage was on a one-way cargo plane to Siberia. I finally got out of her that she'd lost her luggage once flying from San Francisco to Chicago, changing planes in Denver. She did eventually get her bag back, but she was distrustful to this day.

That might explain why her backpack weighed a ton. She'd shoved everything in it instead of her suitcase.

"You can take a nap if you want," I offered as the elevator doors wooshed open. "I need to talk to the event coordinator this afternoon."

"Why would I take a nap? I'm not tired."

Using the key card, I pushed open the door and ushered her inside. "You may not be tired but you're more wound than a long-tailed cat in a room full of rockers, as my grandmother used to say. You may want to hit the minibar."

Like a tiny tornado, Ashlyn rounded on me after dropping her backpack on the couch. "I am not—"

She broke off and heaved a huge sigh, rubbing her hands over her face.

"Okay, I am stressed," she admitted. "There's something you need to know about me. I'm not a good traveler."

I feigned shock and horror. "You're kidding. Are you sure? Because I never would have noticed."

Ashlyn flipped me off and then fell back onto the sofa, propping her feet on the glass coffee table. I could already see that she was relaxing now that we had arrived at our destination.

"Asshole. Seriously, I don't travel well because I'm something of a control freak. Just a little one, though."

"A little control freak?" I simply had to know more about this. I'd seen a few signs here and there but nothing too awful. "How little?"

She buried her face in her hands with a groan and then finally peeked up at me through her fingers.

"If they would have let me fly the plane, I would have."

"You have a pilot's license?"

I really was learning about her.

"No."

And some of it was seriously weird. But cute.

"You don't have a pilot's license? Then I'm not sure why you'd think we would be safer with you flying the plane. Seems like it would be the opposite."

"It's not always logical."

"Clearly. In the spirit of sharing personal little anecdotes about each other I think you should know that I do, indeed, have my pilot's license and I would never have thought to try and land that huge aircraft."

"You have your pilot's license?"

I wasn't sure if I should find her tone insulting or charming. I decided on the latter because she's had a rough morning.

"I do. It was on my bucket list. Along with climbing that mountain."

"Someday you need to show me that bucket list."

"How about I show you around our digs for the next four days?"

I'd stayed in this hotel a few years ago when I'd also spoken at the convention. It was a beautiful property right on the Gulf of Mexico and I'd made sure that our room had an amazing view. I'd already had a fantasy of the two of us drinking champagne as we watched the sunset.

We might both be naked, too.

Yes, I'm a horndog and I'm completely ashamed of myself. But what could I say? We were a new couple in that first rush of love and sex.

It was an absolutely gorgeous and warm sunny day, so different than what we were used to back home. When we'd left central Illinois, the temperature had been hovering around twelve fucking degrees with a wind chill of zero. Zero. Fahrenheit. That's some ball-shriveling cold and I was glad that we had a short respite from it.

There weren't many people on the beach below, but the glistening emerald green waters seem to go on forever, beckoning to us to jump in and splash about. We needed two beach chairs, a couple of fruity rum drinks, and a good spot under the fronds of a palm tree.

Ashlyn loved the view from the windows and balcony and she did all the appropriate oohing and ahhing, but when she really went crazy was when she saw the bathtub. It was big enough for four – maybe five – although I was hoping she'd want to keep it just us. With a giggle, she hopped right into the tub, clothes still on.

She'd kicked off her shoes in the bedroom.

"You know I have a jetted tub at home," I reminded her, watching indulgently as she stretched out, her hands over her head. She was so petite she couldn't reach from one end to the other. I loved it when she was like this, her passion for life and fun boundless. For all her no-nonsense business demeanor, she had the cutest goofy streak, too. I loved making her laugh, and I was thinking that I might want to do that for a very long time into the future. She'd easily shaken off her traveling stress, thank goodness. I didn't want anything to get in the way of our vacation. "You've been in it."

"This one is big enough for all three of us."

"Three?"

"You, me, and Sam."

"That's true. We didn't let Sam jump in with us."

"He was mad about that."

That puppy had pouted the entire time Ashlyn and I were in that bathtub. He'd ruined any romantic vibe we might have had going. He just kept staring at us with his big brown eyes and whining every few minutes.

"He wasn't too happy about me leaving him with George, but I got a text while we were driving here to the hotel. George sent me a picture of Sam sitting on the couch eating breakfast, watching cartoons, and looking pretty damn happy. I think he's settled right in."

She smiled and my heart flipped over in my chest. I doubted that I would ever get used to how beautiful she was. I could barely believe she was in my life. Because of an old creaky elevator. "I miss him already."

"I do too, but he's going to be fine. Sam and George will be best buds by the time we get back." I sat down on the edge of the tub and leaned down to give her a kiss. Her lips were soft and she hooked her arm around my neck, trying to wrestle me into the tub. I wanted to give in, but I had to take care of business first. "I can't take a bath with you now, but if you can wait we can do that when I get back from my meeting."

Sticking out her lower lip in the most adorable pout, Ashlyn sighed. "If I must. I think that I'll kill some time exploring, if you're okay with that."

"I'm fine with it. Have some fun and we'll meet back here about three. We can take a soak and then order room service. Or if you prefer I'll take you somewhere fancy."

I already knew what she'd choose. Ashlyn was a homebody at heart. She liked to get dressed up on occasion, but she was just as happy to hang around the house in one of my old t-shirts.

"Whatever you want." She held out her hand and I lifted her from the bathtub, placing her dainty feet down on the tile floor. I kept my arms around her, pulling her close and pressing a kiss on her neck. She smelled delicious. My will to leave and get my business done was weak. I kept picturing her in a sexy bikini on the beach. "I might grab a bite to eat. I don't think I can wait until dinner. Aren't you hungry?"

Shaking that image from my brain, I tried to focus on the here and now. We could play later. "I had a huge breakfast when we were delayed, remember?"

I didn't mention that she'd probably worked up an appetite with all the pacing she'd done. She wriggled in my arms, trying to get free.

"If you don't go do your stuff, you won't be free later."

Reluctantly I let her go, instantly missing how she felt in my arms. I was pathetic and addicted to this woman, but I was deliriously happy. So there.

"You're right, I suppose."

She rolled her eyes at my sad sack expression.

"I'm sending you off to a business meeting in a semitropical paradise, not off to war. Those sad puppy eyes aren't working on me."

I'd have to ask Sam what his secret was. She fell for his every time.

I leaned down so we were nose to nose. "You're mean."

"You love it. Now get going. How can I miss you if you never go away?"

Cracking up, I managed to steal another kiss. "I do love it. Have fun while I'm gone. Call me if you need me."

We walked together out of the bathroom, through the bedroom, and toward the door. The room was drenched in sunshine and it made a halo around Ashlyn's golden hair, the light reflecting off the silky tresses. She was far from angelic. She ought to have devil horns. "I think I can manage to entertain myself for a few hours. But just in case, you have bail money, right?"

"Absolutely."

If the beginning of this trip was any indication, this was going to be a fantastic four days.

CHAPTER NINETEEN

Ashlyn

THE NEXT MORNING Kyle was kicking off the convention with his keynote address, a speech he'd been practicing in the mirror this morning while he shaved.

And then when he was buttoning his shirt.

And slipping on his shoes.

And drinking his coffee.

He never mentioned being nervous, but I noticed that he didn't eat any breakfast, sticking to two cups of coffee and simply nibbling on a piece of bacon. When it was time to go downstairs, he hadn't even eaten half of it.

It was strange to see him on "work mode" but it was impressive, too. He didn't say much, seemingly inside of his head preparing for his speech. He did try and smile at me a few times, but he was clearly not completely present. I tried to be as quiet and soothing as I could but let's face it… I wasn't a *soothing* kind of person. But I gave it my best effort because what he was about to do was a big deal.

Plus, I had my own worries to deal with, and I was doing my best to hide them. He didn't need to be concerned about me right before doing something this important.

The official-looking man that had come up to the suite to escort us downstairs had said that the media was already in the ballroom to cover the event. Just that word *media* had me shaking in my expensive high heels.

Now I was as nervous as Kyle was. My hand shook as we entered the elevator, but Kyle must have had an inkling because he grabbed it and gave me a reassuring smile.

"You don't have to go if you don't want to. You'll probably find it boring."

"Nothing you do could bore me. I'm really looking forward to it."

He paused for a moment and then nodded. "I'm sure I could bore you but there's something else to think about. There will be photographers there."

We'd talked about this. More than once. As Kyle Lewis's girlfriend I was going to be the object of much scrutiny and the world wouldn't always be kind about it. The internet was a rough neighborhood and I knew that I was opening myself up to being criticized for even breathing, let alone having the audacity to date him.

He'd warned me that they'd take my picture, try and get a quote, and maybe even follow me around. They'd splash those photos all over the papers and the internet, and some of the more smarmy journalists wouldn't bother with the truth, details, or anything like research.

We'd been shielded in Arborville, but out here in the big bad world Kyle was a press event wherever he went and whatever he said. That was his reality and if I wanted to be in his world I'd have to deal with it, too. Emmy had told me that I needed to grow a thick skin quickly. I'd always thought that I didn't much care what others thought about me, but as the light on the elevator panel ascended down I was beginning to think that I was wrong.

Floor four. Three. Two…Lobby. Shit, too late now.

I drew a shaky breath and smoothed down the black and navy blue dress I'd bought for just this occasion. It looked business-like without being boring and I'd paired it with a pair of black pumps and a few pieces of discreet silver jewelry. Even my hair was tamed today and pulled back in a large barrette. I wanted to look cool, calm, and capable. No rock band t-shirts, no ripped jeans and Converse tennis shoes. This would be the first impression the world had of me and I wanted to make Kyle proud.

Yep, I admit it.

"It will be fine. It's all good." I squeezed his hand, my palms damp. "Just don't let go."

"I won't. Don't give them anything. They'll yell out questions but act like you don't hear them. Just smile and look forward. Got it?"

We'd gone over this last night, but I nodded as if it was the first time he'd said it. I wasn't famous but I was dating someone who was. I was going to have to get used to this if Kyle and I stayed together.

I fervently hoped we could make this work.

The first few steps out of the elevator weren't that bad. With my hand in Kyle's we walked down a cramped hallway and then turned to the left. That's when it all hit me.

It was like a wave of sound and energy coming at us all at

once, and for a moment I paused, almost stumbling back but then Kyle put his arm around my waist, his hold strong and reassuring. I could do this if I didn't have to do it alone.

There were dozens of reporters, including a couple of television cameras. For some reason I hadn't expected that. The incessant clicking of the cameras was muted by the yelling of the reporters each hoping to hear something they could report. Even one quote would have done for them. They pelted question after question at us, unrelenting as we walked the gauntlet being held back by security. Nothing was off limits and I flinched when a man asked about "the pretty girl", which I guess was supposed to be me.

Just as Kyle had coached me, I walked quickly and kept my gaze forward. A smile was frozen on my lips and my heart pounded against my ribs painfully. The blood roared in my ears but even that couldn't drown out the noise in the lobby. I had no idea how Kyle could do this on a regular basis.

As fast as it had started it was over.

We were standing in a small room adjacent to the larger one where Kyle would be giving his speech. I could breathe slightly easier now, although my knees were mostly jelly. I would be glad to sit down and just listen.

"You're on in ten," the man with the clipboard said. "Water?"

Kyle smiled and nodded. "That would be great. And one for Ashlyn too, please?"

A cold plastic bottle magically appeared in my hand and this time Kyle did let go so he could open it for me. "You did great. Are you okay?"

I needed a drink, but I didn't want to smear my lipstick. Would there be more pictures taken later or during? I didn't know.

"I'm fine," I replied and I actually sounded it, to my great relief. "That was…something."

Wincing, Kyle took a drink of his water. "They're hoping for a quote about the new AI software. They won't get it."

I realized I didn't really know what he was talking about. We spoke about his work in sort of a peripheral way but not with any specificity. Mostly because I didn't understand it but now I had to wonder if there was another reason. Did he not talk about it because he didn't think I'd like it? Once more I was thrown into a swamp of uncertainty. Kyle and I were a million miles apart, not only in the way we looked at life but in how we lived it. The press sure as hell didn't follow me around, but he lived his life in the public eye.

A fact I was only now beginning to fully comprehend.

There was far more separating us than simply how we viewed the past or the future. A part of his life was public and probably always would be. If I wanted to be in his life, I'd have to share him to a certain extent, and I'd have to open myself up to people as well.

Could I do it? I wasn't sure.

Was Kyle worth it? Yes.

Did that make it easier? Sadly, no.

Kyle

I WOULDN'T SAY it was the greatest presentation that I'd ever made. Far from it actually. I wasn't prepared to make any statements regarding my current project and that's what they really wanted to hear about. I talked about a few others that I'd recently finished but weren't big news, and I also spoke about the potential benefits which I completely believed in.

Every now and then I would look down into the audience and see Ashlyn sitting in the front row. It felt so right that she was here with me, by my side. A team. She'd managed the press like a veteran, much better than I had when I'd first captured their attention. I wished that I could stop the nastiness and troll-like behavior on the internet that she was going to receive but I didn't have that kind of power. The best thing I could do was try to keep her away from it and support her when I couldn't.

When my presentation was over I took a few questions from the audience, much to the chagrin of the organizers. They'd warned me that they couldn't control what might be asked but I wasn't worried about that. There was always some arrogant kid in the audience that thought he was smarter than me. What that kid didn't realize is that there was *always* someone smarter. Always someone else nipping at my heels. I was only as good as my last project and others were trying to elbow me aside every day.

That's how it was supposed to be. The competition pushed us forward even if I, personally, was knocked back.

After about half a dozen questions, the organizer smoothly

stood and called the presentation to close. The last query for me about the effect of AI on humankind was clearly enough for the poor man. Security hustled me back into the small room, pressing a fresh and cold bottle of water into my hand.

The organizer shook my hand and patted me on the back, all smiles. The others in the room were all happy as well so I must have done a halfway decent job out there.

I felt a hand on my arm and looked down to see Ashlyn standing next to me, a smile on her face.

"You did great. Amazing. Awesome. And all of those other cool adjectives."

I'd done my job today and now I wanted nothing more than to spend some time with her. I leaned down to whisper in her ear.

"What do you say we get out of here?"

CHAPTER TWENTY

Ashlyn

KYLE HAD ARRANGED time in the spa for me the next day while he worked. It was absolutely decadent but so relaxing to be massaged, exfoliated, and moisturized within an inch of my life. After all of that pampering it wasn't over, however. I had my hair styled and my makeup done all while getting a mani-pedi.

I felt like a freakin' princess.

But I'd better not get too used to it. I doubted my sparkly eyeshadow would go with my normal everyday jeans and t-shirts. Or maybe they would. It was worth a try.

As I was packing up to leave the spa, I was handed a large box by the hairdresser. She was wearing a huge grin so I knew it was something good.

A dress. A sapphire blue cocktail dress, sleeveless and beaded around the neckline and hem. Rather modest in the front but definitely sexy with its scandalously low back. I didn't know what he had planned but I couldn't wait. Carefully, I slipped it on, not wanting to mess up my hair and makeup. Pulling up the side zip, I glanced in the mirror and the woman staring back at me was glowing and happy, practically vibrating with excitement. She was in love. It was that obvious and I couldn't help but wonder if he could see it. I'd barely begun to admit it to myself but there was no way to deny my own eyes.

I could pretend it wasn't true, but it wouldn't change the reality.

Ashlyn loved Kyle. If we were schoolkids someone would have written it on the face of my locker – *true love 4 ever*.

Slipping on the shoes that had been included in the package, I gathered up my discarded clothing and headed up to our suite. My heart raced with excitement and my steps were quicker than normal despite the precariously high heels. By the time I reached the door to our room, I was breathless. My shaking fingers could barely unlock the door, but Kyle must have heard me on the other side. He pulled it open and stood in the entry looking like the most handsome man I'd ever seen in my life.

Wearing a black tuxedo. Bare feet. I must have caught him when he was dressing.

We were both just staring at each other. Somebody had to say something or I'd be standing in the hallway all evening.

It took a minute, but I found my voice. "Hi."

"Hi. You are so beautiful."

He said wonderful things like that quite a bit but tonight was a little different. There was something in his gaze, a catch in his voice when he said it.

"Thank you. So are you."

That made him chuckle and then he must have realized we were standing in the doorway because he stepped back and bowed low as I entered.

"My lady, welcome to what I hope will be a romantic evening."

We weren't really the type for stuff like this. I was a sweat-pants and t-shirt kind of gal and Kyle loved pizza and beer, so it meant everything that he'd gone all out like this in an attempt to make tonight special.

Didn't he know that all the time I spent with him was spe-cial? I didn't need these candles and the soft music playing in the background. I didn't need the elaborately set table with its white linen tablecloth and napkins, and shiny silver forks and spoons. Even the china gleamed in the flickering candlelight. It was perfect and over the top and my throat clogged with emotion as I imagined him making plans days ago to surprise me.

"This is incredible." He wore a smug grin. "How long have you been planning this?"

"Since you said you would come with me. I wanted to do something really special."

"You succeeded. I didn't expect...this."

He lifted the champagne bottle from the ice bucket. "How about some champagne?"

Not waiting for me to answer, he popped the cap and foam bubbled from the top and into the glass as he poured the golden liquid. It tasted sharp on my tongue and the sparkling bubbles tickled my nose.

"Ashlyn," he began, his gaze trained on his bare feet. "There's so much I want to say—"

He broke off but I stayed quiet, letting him gather his thoughts. My heart slammed into my ribs and I held my breath. It was that kind of moment.

He finally looked up and his eyes were shiny with moisture.

"You've changed so much for me. The last few weeks have been the best of my life."

"For me, too."

The words came out high and squeaky, but I was lucky to be able to say anything at all. I swear I was beginning to sweat right through this fancy dress. If he didn't hurry I was going to collapse on the expensive tile, and they'd have to call an ambulance.

Please say it.

"I've waited a long time to meet a woman like you and I feel so lucky that I have." He took a ragged breath and then placed our glasses on the table next to us before pulling me into his arms. This close he had to know that I was literally shaking like a leaf. I clung to his shoulders, sure I was going to faint at any moment. "What I'm trying to say – and badly – is that I've fallen in love with you, Ashlyn. I hope that's okay."

This wasn't the first time a man had told me he loved me, but it was certainly the most important. Mostly because I loved him back. A lot. More than I ever had. That's when it hit me that I hadn't said it out loud yet and he was probably wondering if I was going to speak.

"I love you, too."

It came out all gravelly and barely audible, but he heard me and understood. His eyes crinkled when he smiled. I hadn't noticed before, but it made him even more attractive and his happiness even more sincere.

I was in so deep with him, at the point of no return.

There was hot food under silver domes, but my appetite wasn't for food. Reaching up, I plucked at the end of his bowtie so the two ends hung loose. One of his eyebrows quirked and that evil smile played on his lips. He called me the devil, but he was the dangerous one.

"Is that a hint?"

I ran my hands up under his jacket so I could push it off his shoulders. I could feel the warmth from his body even through the fabric of his shirt. I wanted to be skin to skin with him as soon as possible.

"Do you need me to be a little more clear?"

He shrugged off the jacket and laid it across the back of a chair. "I'm getting the message loud and clear. I only have one question."

"And that is?"

"Bedroom or dining table?"

He was such a kinky bastard. I knew what he wanted.

"Is there chocolate on any of these trays?"

"There is. Strawberries and dipping chocolate. I also ordered some whipped cream."

"The dining table it is then."

He'd planned it all in advance. He really was a genius.

★ ★ ★

CLOTHES ENDED UP tossed around the room and my beautiful blue cocktail dress had been draped over the arm of a chair. Disgraceful for an item so beautiful and expensive but I'd worry about it later. Right now, I was concentrating on the man between my thighs as I lounged on the dining room table. Kyle was kissing a damp path from my ankles to my thighs and then going back and starting all over again. The heat that had started in my belly was spreading through my veins like melted butter.

He gave me a wicked grin. "I'm glad you left your shoes on."

I hadn't on purpose, only now realizing it when he pointed it out. It was rather kinky and decadent though to see myself naked as the day I was born except for my high heels.

Kissing a trail up my inner thigh and onto my quivering abdomen, Kyle dipped his tongue into my bellybutton, causing my body to bow and my hands to grab onto his biceps to keep the room from spinning out of control. My eyelids were heavy but I forced them to stay open, determined to enjoy looking at my very sexy and incredibly handsome boyfriend. In the buff.

He was muscular but not overly so. He had more of a swimmer's body or perhaps a baseball player. I let my gaze linger on his wide shoulders before allowing it to wander down his chest, over his flat stomach, and then pausing at his hard cock – thick and long and practically crying out for my mouth. I began to sit up but his hands gently pressed me back down onto the table, the shiny oak cool under my feverish skin.

"Easy, honey. I have a hell of a lot of plans for you tonight. We can get to me later."

Who was I to argue?

Leaning over me, he lapped at my nipples until they were hard as diamonds and sending arrows of arousal straight to my clit. I moved restlessly under him but he held me easily in place, using his lips and teeth to drive me slowly out of my mind. Within minutes he had me panting and gasping, clutching the back of his head. I couldn't decide if I wanted him to stop or continue and my brain was beginning to get that sex-fogged feeling where all logical thinking ceased and I functioned purely on emotion.

I was floating on a cloud of dreamy pleasure when his mouth abandoned my breasts and was instead replaced with a warmer liquid. The delicious aroma of chocolate hit my nostrils and I inhaled deeply, the scent a potent aphrodisiac. Blood flew through my veins as if it had golden wings, making a roaring sound in my ears that blocked out the real world. It would be time to go back eventually, but I was happy to stay here where nothing more was asked of me than to enjoy and feel.

I hadn't been paying attention and at some point, Kyle had lifted the silver dome on the chafing dish of warm chocolate. He also unveiled a tray of strawberries and bite-sized cake pieces arranged artfully on an oval tray, and then plucked a juicy red berry, dipping it into the melted goodness.

His smile was delightfully evil and I watched entranced as he ran the chocolate covered strawberry in a circle around a painfully hard nipple and then popped the fruit into his mouth. A trickle of juice ran from the corner of his lips and I lifted up and ran my tongue over it. Sweet and tart, just like the kiss I'd received right after along with a groan of...desire? Frustration? I wasn't sure, but it was sexy as hell.

He repeated his action but this time he placed the ripe fruit at my lips. I bit down into the juicy flesh and the decadent flavor burst on my tongue.

My eyes fluttered closed as he dipped a finger into the chocolate, painting a pattern on my abdomen and then licking it off. Slowly. Deliberately. Taking his own sweet time. His tongue made magic on my sensitive skin and he had me wriggling and giggling underneath him as he tickled at my ribs.

"Hmmm…where should I paint this next?"

His voice rumbled against my hip, sending tremors to my clit. He was only teasing, of course. We both knew where that chocolate was going… I shivered with anticipation, but he wasn't in any hurry, letting a few drops of chocolate fall on my thighs and below my bellybutton.

The hotel room had to be about two hundred degrees or had my flesh gone up in flames? The tip of Kyle's tongue danced playfully along my inner thigh, but he studiously avoided the one place I desperately needed him to go.

I waited, holding my breath for that moment. Electricity zipped up and down my veins, my entire body quivering until I had to reach out and grab the sides of the table to hold myself down. My eyes were squeezed shut and Kyle had gone quiet, not saying a word.

And then the wait was over.

Sticky, warm chocolate dripped onto my clit. Not hot enough to burn but enough that I cried out at the overwhelming sensations that rocketed through me. His tongue was right there licking it off and I immediately went over the edge, calling out his name as he pressed his face between my thighs. Later I would swear that I saw actual honest-to-god fireworks explode behind my lids.

My back arched up off the table as Kyle's strong hands grasped my hips and pulled me toward him, his hard cock pressing at my entrance. I was so ready for him he slid in embarrassingly easy, all the way to the hilt. So full of him it was like he was inside me and all around me at the same time. His body hovered above, his rock-solid arms planted on either side of me, all the while his cock thrust lazily in and out as if we had all the time in the world and I wasn't on fire from the inside out.

Wrapping my legs around his waist, I dug the high heels of my shoes into his firm backside trying to urge him on. "Harder. Faster."

Somehow, I'd managed to get the words out in between panting breaths. Kyle chuckled softly and increased the tempo of his strokes just enough to push me closer to a second orgasm but not enough to get me there.

The bastard.

"Easy, babe. We've got all night."

Clearly, he was speaking for himself.

I reached and wrapped my arms around his neck, twining my fingers into his springy hair and pulling him down for a wet, hot kiss. Blood roared in my ears and I could feel it thundering through my arms and legs, all the way to my toes. The arousal had built in my lower belly and it would go off any minute. If only Kyle would speed the hell up.

"I need you now," I said, my voice hoarse and trembly. "Fuck me harder. I'm so close."

Those must have been the magic words because he did begin to thrust harder and faster, his teeth gritted together and his jaw tight. His fingers tightened on my hips and I would probably have marks there tomorrow, but I didn't care. I was getting exactly what I wanted right now.

Him. All he could give me.

I fought to keep my eyes open this time, wanting to see him

go over as well. Our bodies were covered in a sheen of sweat and the sounds we made were slightly obscene with our grunting and the sound of flesh meeting flesh. I was hovering on the edge, in that shimmery place where the rest of the world melts away and we were the only two people on the planet.

His cock kept running over that sweet spot inside of me and his next stroke was the one that sent me over. The room whirled and spun, blurring in front of my eyes. I couldn't make out Kyle's features clearly, but I knew the exact moment he climaxed by the sexy growl that burst from his lips along with my name. A few seconds later he collapsed on top of me, our damp, sticky bodies pressed together.

Running my fingers through his hair, I didn't say anything. There weren't any words for a moment like this. We'd said them before and then our lovemaking had placed an exclamation point on the end. We'd had sex before but tonight it felt different. Closer and more intimate. I could be myself with him and not worry that he might think I was too bold or slutty. I was accepted and loved, a feeling I'd never had until this man.

I never wanted to let it go.

Eventually he looked up at me, a playful grin on his face. "I think we missed dinner."

I was as wanton as the next woman but even I couldn't eat dinner on this table after our romp. I just couldn't.

"We could order a pizza."

"You get the shower going and I'll call it in."

That was a deal I could get on board with.

CHAPTER TWENTY-ONE

Ashlyn

ALL GOOD THINGS had to come to an end. Four days on a warm beach was utterly fantastic but we both had responsibilities. We couldn't spend the rest of our lives sipping rum drinks and getting a tan.

No matter how much we wanted to.

We both fell asleep on the flight home and I continued that trend while Kyle drove us from the airport to Arborville. When the car stopped, I woke and yawned sleepily, stretching my arms over my head and looking around. My condo looked the same as did the snow-covered yard. The only differences were the dark green sedan in my driveway and all the lights on inside. I'd left one lamp on a timer in the front window.

That's not right.

Rubbing the sleep out of my eyes, I shook my head trying to take in the scene before me. It was dark out so maybe Kyle had driven me to the wrong house.

"How long were we in Florida?" I asked.

"Four days, I swear." He popped the trunk where the luggage was. "Why don't you give me your keys and let me go inside? You stay here."

"Dude, there is no way I'm going to let you walk in there by yourself. Maybe I should call 911?"

Now that I was shaking off the fog of sleep my mind was beginning to actually function. The car wasn't familiar, but this scenario was giving me serious deja vu. This wasn't the first time I'd come home and found all my lights on.

Oh crap.

"I think I know who is in my house."

"One of your friends?"

"Nope, my grandmother."

There was a tiny pause before he responded.

"Your grandmother the United States senator?"

"That very one. I think the car is a rental."

"Then we shouldn't keep her waiting. I'll get the bags."

I hadn't even thought about introducing Kyle to Gran this early in our relationship, but fate had taken a hand and here we were.

Just one big happy family.

★ ★ ★

Kyle

HEAVING THE LUGGAGE out of the back of the car, I slammed the trunk shut. After four days in Florida, I was fucking freezing and couldn't wait to get inside where there might be heat and shelter from the cold wind. It looked like it had snowed some more while we were gone.

"I should warn you that she can be difficult. She's used to getting her own way and when she doesn't, she thinks she can negotiate a settlement somewhere in between. I put it down to being in Congress."

Interesting perspective. I hadn't noticed our elected lawmakers negotiating or compromising on anything the last several years. But hey, I might be wrong.

I did appreciate a strong-willed woman though, especially since I was dating one. I was anxious to meet Ashlyn's grandmother and wanted to make a good impression. I'd seen the senator on television several times and she always appeared to be passionately advocating for her constituents and working to make her state a better place. I wasn't strongly political but that seemed like what we paid our representatives to do.

"I can't wait to meet your grandmother," I assured Ashlyn as she unlocked the front door. "I can't stay long, though. I have to go pick up Sam from George's place."

"You'll give him a kiss and hug from me?"

"George or Sam?" I teased, placing her suitcase and backpack on the floor in the foyer. The whole house was lit up like an airport runway. Clearly the senator wasn't worried about conserving energy. Perhaps she was afraid to be on her own after dark so she'd turned on all the lights. "I ask because I'm not kissing George. You'll have to do it yourself."

Ashlyn didn't laugh at my joke, however. Her attention was drawn to the far side of the living room and my gaze followed hers. A white-haired woman about Ashlyn's height was standing there in a lavender jogging suit and big pink fuzzy slippers.

Senator Roslyn Caldwell.

I recognized her from "Meet the Press". She held out her arms, her smile widening, and Ashlyn flew into them. A loving reunion that I was happy to witness. Moving forward, I held out my hand to greet the older woman as her gaze fell upon me.

She was still smiling but her gaze was appraising, looking me up and down and deciding if she approved of me. I'd had worse from distrustful parents. I could do this and win her over.

"Hi, I'm Kyle Lewis, Ashlyn's boyfriend. It's a pleasure to meet you, Senator Caldwell."

"It's nice to meet you, young man. I didn't realize Ashlyn was seeing anyone."

Clearly, I was a surprise.

"I was going to tell you, Gran, when I visited next month." Ashlyn reached up and hugged her grandmother again. "Why didn't you call? I could have had Emmy or Shelby meet you at the airport."

"I rented a car. I am capable of that despite my advanced age. As for calling, it was a spontaneous decision to come. I didn't know if I would be able to get away until last night. I flew in this morning. Now where have you been, child? You look tan."

Advanced age? Roslyn Caldwell radiated energy and vitality. I wouldn't want to meet her in a dark alley. From what I'd seen tonight and on television, she might wrestle alligators for relaxation.

Giggling, Ashlyn shook her head and then took my hand, giving me a loving look. Thank goodness, she'd remembered that we were supposed to be in love. "We were in Florida for a tech convention. Kyle was the keynote speaker. I'm surprised you didn't see it in the news."

It was clear from the senator's expression that she'd known who I was before I walked into the house. She must have seen the photos online.

"Actually, I did see it. One of my aides gave me a transcript of the speech but I haven't had a chance to read it yet. I am looking forward to it."

"I hope you enjoy it."

She turned her attention back to Ashlyn.

"You're probably wondering why I'm here unannounced."

If Ashlyn wasn't, I was.

"Is everything okay, Gran? Are you sick?"

Roslyn Caldwell snorted. "Sick? Germs are terrified of me. No, I'm not sick. I'm here to help you."

I had a bad feeling about this. Really bad. My radar was picking up on some bad mojo.

"Help me?" Ashlyn echoed, her brows pinched together. "What do you mean?"

"With my help, we'll turn that town council around and squash this technical campus idea. Together we can do it."

This was going to be awkward.

CHAPTER TWENTY-TWO

Ashlyn

I PRACTICALLY PUSHED Kyle out of the door, begging him with my eyes not to engage with my grandmother. He'd gone reluctantly. I could see that he wanted to discuss the technical campus and tell her all the wonderful reasons that it should be built, but he didn't know Roslyn Caldwell. It wasn't easy to get her to change her mind, but I'd had much more practice at it.

Of course, the open question was…

Did I *want* her to change her mind?

While the relationship between Kyle and I had changed, my thoughts on the location for the campus hadn't. I wanted those old homes saved and if my grandmother could make that happen, I wasn't exactly against that.

I wasn't against Kyle, either. I'd shown him other options for the location. He'd said they weren't as good but were they *good enough*? I didn't know. I also didn't want a war between the two people I loved most. That I was sure of.

"You certainly surprised me," I said after watching the tail-lights of Kyle's car disappear into the night. "I didn't think I'd see you until Easter."

"You act like you're not happy to see me. If you'd returned

my messages you would have known I was coming."

Gran had never been one for small talk or inane pleasantries. I'd always admired that about her and even now it made it easier. We weren't going to pretend or tiptoe around the subject. Straight and to the point. That's what she'd always say to me when I was growing up.

"I am happy to see you. I'm just not sure I'm as happy about the reason you're here."

"Why didn't you tell me you were dating Kyle Lewis?"

Turning from the front window, I padded on sock feet into the kitchen. "I'm going to make some hot chocolate. Do you want some?"

"If whiskey isn't a choice, then yes. Are you going to answer my question?"

"Yes, but I'm going to get this started first." I poured milk into a saucepan. "I didn't tell you I was dating Kyle because I rarely tell you about my dates, Gran."

"Until you get serious with one," Gran agreed with a nod. "So you're not serious about this one?"

"I am," I admitted, stirring the sugar and cocoa into the milk. "But that's a recent development and I hadn't had a chance to tell you yet. Kyle's amazing. You're going to love him."

Because hating him simply wasn't an option. If anything, Kyle and my grandmother had much in common. Both driven and ambitious but loving with the people around them.

"I'm sure that I will but there is the open question of where the technical campus will be built."

I poured the hot chocolate into two mugs and handed one to Gran. "Kyle and I have talked this subject to death. He's researched this back and forth and he assures me that the houses are too old and rundown to be saved. He says that they're a hazard and that someone could get hurt. He's having structural engineer see if one or two can be saved and he might restore those and make them part of the campus."

Gran took a sip of her cocoa and then sat down at the table. "What if the engineers say that none of them can be saved? Or all them?"

Warily, I sat down at the table across from Gran. "I don't know but at this point it doesn't matter. The town council has given him and his company preliminary permission to start planning. Of course, they'll want to approve the final design and such."

"Of course. But why leave it up to your boyfriend? What if we could change the council's mind? What if we could get those homes saved?"

"That's a lot of what-ifs, Gran."

"You have to think big. Do you really want to save those homes?"

Yes, but I also didn't want to throw all my energies into a project that wasn't going to pan out from the beginning. If the houses were in as bad shape as Kyle believed, I'd be wasting my time.

"I do, but they may not be able to be saved. That's what he's waiting on."

"We could get our own engineers."

I doubted they'd be any better than Kyle's. I was sure he'd hired the best.

"Even if they say something different, it would be expensive to restore the homes."

Gran shrugged. "We could do fundraisers, get a few corporate sponsors. Arborville needs to make an investment of their own, of course. It would be the town that would reap the benefits in more tourists."

My grandmother had been in Washington DC too long, I think.

"Gran, when you say Arborville what you really mean is the taxpayers. You want the taxpayers to pay to restore the houses. What do they get in return?"

"They would get to brag that they had a restored historic district and it just might bring in money and tourists. But what I meant was that Arborville will take control of the restoration, not necessarily pay for it. Why are you arguing with me about this, Ashlyn Rose? You said this is what you wanted the last time we spoke. Now I'm here to help you."

"That was before—"

I broke off when I saw the expression on Gran's face. Sour. She looked...sour.

"You mean before you met Kyle Lewis."

"No, before I talked with him about this project. I don't want the taxpayers to be on the hook for tens of millions of dollars and I don't think you do, either. Or do you?"

"The town will find investors other than Kyle Lewis. I have a few connections that can help."

There was no doubt in my mind that Gran knew a bunch of wealthy people. She'd be in politics long enough and she's traveled and hobnobbed with the filthy rich all over the world. But that didn't mean any of them wanted to invest in a small town in the middle of cows and corn.

"You sound like you have a plan."

She sat back, a satisfied smile on her face. "I do. Stop worrying about the money. When we're done here, people will be lined up to pay for the restoration. Maybe even your young man."

Gran was being incredibly optimistic.

"I doubt that very much."

"Then someone else will. You seem quite taken with this man, Ashlyn. Your grandfather wanted me to give up the law to stay home and cook and clean, but I couldn't do it. Are you thinking that you're going to give up what you believe in because you might be in love? That doesn't sound like you, and it's not how I raised you."

It didn't sound like me and it certainly wasn't how I'd been raised.

"I'm just being practical."

"Practically a doormat," Gran scoffed, her brows raised. "You've just folded your tent and given up. All for a man. A man far different from yourself. I brought you up to respect the past. He doesn't respect anything but science and technology."

"That's not true," I denied hotly. "You don't even know Kyle. He's not like that. He has a great respect for the past."

"So much respect that he's going to take a wrecking ball to an entire city block of historic homes? You have a funny way of defining respect, Ashlyn."

"You're twisting my words. I'm not your political opponent, I'm your granddaughter. This isn't about winning."

"I want you to be happy. Is it so terrible that I have doubts about whether you'd be happy with Kyle Lewis?"

"You've never liked any of my boyfriends."

Not a one, in fact.

"Because your taste in men is questionable. Can you honestly look me in the eye and say that you and Kyle Lewis have a future? That you can make it work?"

I had been thinking that, but clearly Gran thought I was either crazy or dumb. Maybe both.

"I think that I'm a grown woman and can make these decisions for myself."

"Good," Gran pronounced with a firm nod. "Then you can decide whether you want to give up the fight for those homes."

I was smack dab in the middle of a hot mess.

CHAPTER TWENTY-THREE

Kyle

WHEN I PICKED up Sam last night, George had assured me that I just needed a good night's sleep in my own bed. I'd feel better and this entire situation wouldn't look like a huge fuckup.

He was a big old liar.

I didn't feel any better and I'd already had a large coffee and a lemon poppyseed muffin. Normally, that was enough to put me in a great mood.

Sam, on the other hand, was thrilled that I was home and had taken to following me around the house even more than usual, just in case I decided to make a break for Florida again. I'd almost tripped over him several times this morning.

"You lied to me," I stated to George the minute he showed up at the house. "Are your pants on fire?"

Languidly, he turned to check the back of his jeans as he entered and headed straight for the kitchen. "Don't think so. What did I lie about? If I did though, I'm sure it was for your own good."

"You told me it would be better this morning. It's not."

George retrieved a soda can from the fridge and popped it

open. "I did say that. Is Ashlyn not answering your texts?"

"She's answered them."

"Then what's so terrible? Did she break up with you?"

"No."

"Did she tell you that you're a horrible man and she hates you?"

"No."

"But everything isn't better? She's still your girlfriend. That has to count for something. That woman hasn't talked her out of dating you."

"That *woman* is her grandmother. We need to be respectful."

Flipping open his briefcase, George pulled out a single sheet of paper. "Are you sure we have to be? Because when you read that you might not feel so kindly toward the old battle axe."

I wasn't sure what I was looking at and I was so distracted it was difficult to concentrate.

"What am I looking at?"

"That is a copy of a city permit. Senator Caldwell received that last week. Tuesday, to be exact. She's going to have a demonstration at the location of those old houses on the twenty-first. When you told me she was in town, I called a contact in the mayor's office this morning. He gave me that."

Tuesday. She'd had the permit since *Tuesday*. That was before Ashlyn and I left for Florida.

"She said she just came into town yesterday."

George shrugged. "She might have. She probably has a huge staff of aides to do admin work like this."

"So she knew she was going to come to Arborville. It wasn't as last minute as she made it sound."

"Yep." He pulled another piece of paper from his briefcase and held it out. "This is why I'm so late today. You need to see this. I called in a couple of favors to get that."

"This looks like polling results."

"It is. That's the latest poll results between Senator Caldwell and the nominee from the other party. She's down five points. If you read more closely through that, people said they thought she was out of touch with rural hometown America."

"Like Arborville," I finished for him. "You're saying that she's doing this to raise her poll numbers? That's crazy talk, man. She's here to help her one and only granddaughter."

"I'm sure she is. But this will help her too, Kyle."

I couldn't believe it.

"Some small town gathering about some houses? I doubt it. No one will ever even know."

George laughed and plopped down on my sofa, Sam jumping up next to him. "I love that you remain above the political fray but sometimes that makes you incredibly naive, my friend. I didn't come here without doing my homework. I called a few of the larger hotels in town. They're completely booked starting the twentieth. By who? Let me tell you before you even ask. The press. National press. She's using this – and you, by the way – to up her poll numbers. What is more homespun than going after the big, bad millionaire that programs robots taking everyone's job?"

"I don't do that," I said, desperation in my tone. This sounded like a clusterfuck in the making. How could I get it cancelled? "I don't take people's jobs. I create jobs."

"I bet that's not how she's going to make it sound. Listen,

I've already called in our PR firm and they're on this. But you better be, too. She's playing to win. Are you?"

Yes. No. Wait. What about Ashlyn?

"Do you think Ashlyn knows?"

"Doubtful. Do you?"

I thought about it for a moment but then shook my head. There was no way she had any clue as to what her beloved grandmother was up to.

"No, no way. I think she thinks that the senator is truly here to help her."

"And she may be. But she's also thinking about using this for herself. You? You're not in the equation, my friend. In fact, you may be in the way. She might be telling Ashlyn right this minute that she could do a hell of a lot better than you."

This was bad. So very bad.

Frankly, the location for the technical center simply wasn't this important. I could relocate it if I truly needed to and it was looking like it was becoming more of a distraction.

"Remember when I told you to look again at those other locations?"

"I do."

"Let's pick one. Nip all of this in the bud. We can tell the town council today that we're passing on the first location. It will make Ashlyn happy and she won't be caught in this tug of war between me and her grandmother."

"The engineering report should come in soon. You don't want to wait?"

I shook my head, my mind already thinking about the possibilities of a new location. "There's no reason to wait. It's a moot point. I'll tell Ashlyn after we talk to the town council and get their tentative okay."

George reached into his briefcase and pulled out a thick file folder. "That will probably be tomorrow. You know if we pick another location that it will delay the project?"

"I know. We'll deal with it."

"I just wanted to make sure."

I was completely sure. It was the one action I could take to keep the peace between myself, Ashlyn, and her grandmother. In the end, it was just land.

★   ★   ★

AFTER A FITFUL night of sleep I'd called in emergency reinforcements. Shelby and Emmy showed up at my shop with coffee and bear claws. Katie shooed us into the back room with a promise to take care of the store while I handled my crisis. She'd taken one look at my face when I showed up at the store and started trying to feed me chocolate at nine in the morning.

Shelby stood and paced back and forth while Emmy and I sat at the tiny table surrounded by cardboard boxes. "Now let's start from the beginning. Where is your grandmother right now?"

"At home," I said with a sigh. "Sitting on my couch and talking on her phone to one of her aides about the rally."

Gran had told me about the rally last night and I'd almost gone catatonic at the news. A month ago, I would have been thrilled but now it sounded like a really good way to push Kyle out of my life.

Emmy groaned and shook her head. "This is not good. Have you told Kyle yet?"

I held up my phone. "Not yet and I need to. I don't want him blindsided by the news."

"So you have talked to him today?" Shelby asked, pausing her pacing. "How did he sound?"

"He sounded fine. Pretty normal. He avoided talking about Gran which I understood. I asked about Sam and we talked about whether I would be free for dinner tonight."

"What did you say?" Emmy asked.

"I said I should probably stay home with Gran since she's visiting."

Shelby nodded as she paced. "That makes sense, but you do have to tell him. Did you finish the book, by the way?"

Shit. She was like a dog with a bone.

"No, but I sincerely doubt you have a chapter devoted to when a girl's grandmother and boyfriend go head to head against the city council."

"Not specifically, but I do have a chapter about when a family doesn't like your boyfriend. Or when they don't get along. But honestly, that's not the issue here."

It wasn't?

"What do you think the issue is?"

I was dying to know because then I could fix it.

"The issue is you."

Damn, that's what I was afraid of.

"Me?" I feigned innocence. "Whatever are you talking about?"

Emmy snorted and laughed. "You crack me up, Ash. Like you don't know."

"I don't. Enlighten me as to how I'm the issue."

"You want it all," Shelby replied, crossing her arms over her chest and giving me a look that she might have given to a third-grader. "You want Kyle, you want love, you want the houses to remain, you want your gran to be happy, and you want all of this without anyone getting upset. Is that about right?"

"You make it sound so unrealistic. You're such a pessimist."

"It is unrealistic," Emmy said when Shelby's face went an unattractive shade of red. I'd royally pissed her off. "And you know it. You just might have to decide. What do you want more? The houses or Kyle?"

"What about Gran?"

Shelby shoved a piece of bear claw into her mouth. "What about her? She has her own life and she only swoops in a couple of times a year, throws your life into chaos, and then flies off. You need to worry about you, not her. She can take care of herself just fine."

I didn't much like Shelby's characterization of Gran but in the last several years that had become more and more true. Even when I was a child, Gran had been about her career as an attorney, trying to take high profile cases that received lots of press.

"She's growing older."

Emmy's brows shot up. "We all are. I saw her on CNN a few weeks ago. She ripped a journalist to shreds without a moment of remorse. I think she's doing fine. This is about you, so stop obfuscating. Which do you want more?"

"I want both," I admitted. "Kyle said he might be able to save a few of the houses."

"And if he can't?" Emmy queried. "Then what was the plan?"

"That I deal with it. I trust that he's looked into it. It's just that…"

I hadn't yet mentioned what my grandmother had said last night.

"Just?" Shelby prompted. "Spill it."

"Gran said that there might be a way to save the houses. She said that she could get investors to do the renovations."

"But Kyle would have to relocate his technical campus," Emmy said with a knowing nod. "How would he take the news?"

"He'd be upset but then I think he'd be okay. It's not about the location to him. It's about the campus."

The one thing I could count on from Kyle is that he would be pragmatic about setbacks. He'd had plenty in his career and they hadn't held him back. If anything, they'd made him even more determined.

"I'll ask you straight out," Shelby said. "Do you want to stop your grandmother from having this rally?"

That wasn't an easy question.

"It doesn't matter what I want. She has all sorts of plans and the press is supposed to be there, too." I took a deep breath and let it out slowly, trying to calm my jangled nerves. "Listen, I admit that I want the houses to stay but I don't think that a big, loud rally is going to help the situation. I tried to talk Gran into just talking to some of these rich people who might want to invest in the project, but she said that they won't pay it any attention until it gets major press."

"So the rally is going forward," Emmy said. "Will you be there?"

"I think I have to be." My gaze bounced between my two best friends. "I was kind of hoping you both would be as well."

"I can't. I have a party on the twenty-first," Emmy said. "I'll have to hear about it later."

"I'll be there," Shelby vowed. "Wild horses couldn't keep me away. Now…are you ready to tell Kyle? Because you don't want him to hear this from anyone else."

"I'm not ready but I'll call him anyway."

It was going to be fine. Everything was going to work out for the best.

But first I had to tell the man I loved that my grandmother was going to make him find another location for his dream project.

This ought to go over well.

CHAPTER TWENTY-FOUR

Ashlyn

I N AN EFFORT to bring Kyle and my grandmother closer I decided to host a little dinner party with the three of us plus our friends – Shelby, Brad, Emmy, and George. I even encouraged Kyle to bring Sam as well since no one could stay cranky around a cute puppy. I wanted everyone to get along tonight and have a good time. Mostly I wanted Gran to cut Kyle some slack and have a more open mind.

It didn't look like that was going to happen.

Kyle didn't bring Sam to dinner but he did bring George, an affable man who was a veritable encyclopedia of information regarding sports. Brad had taken up the challenge to try and find a question that George couldn't answer, and the two of them were having a grand old time discussing baseball players through the twentieth century. It was just good to see Brad off of his phone. When he was like this we could all see why Shelby had fallen for him.

Emmy was in the kitchen lending me a hand but to be honest, most of the cooking was being done by Kyle. He was frying chicken in a heavy cast iron skillet exactly the way his mom had taught him and the smells that were wafting through the house were mouthwatering. Emmy had already made him promise to give her the recipe. She and I were working on the sides including a fruit salad, mashed potatoes, and green peas. Shelby had brought a lemon bundt cake for dessert.

Gran was…supervising.

Perched on a chair in the kitchen, she hadn't said much for the last thirty minutes or so.

That worried me. Instead she'd sipped her chardonnay and watched us work, only speaking when she was asked a question. It was like waiting for the other shoe to drop. She'd glowered at Kyle when he'd arrived, thrown a few barbed questions at him, and then retreated to the bedroom to make a phone call. When she'd returned, she'd taken up her position where she could watch us and even now I could feel her eyes following Kyle's every move. She was studying him, measuring him up, and deciding if he was good enough for me.

It had never occurred to my grandmother to wonder whether I was good enough for *him*.

"You don't mind being in the kitchen, Kyle?"

There it was. The first salvo. I tensed and had the sudden urge to throw myself onto the grenade, but Kyle clearly wasn't perturbed in the least. He was still smiling and whistling as if it was all peachy.

"Not at all, Senator. I find cooking after a long day relaxing. How about you?"

Lord love him for trying to get a conversation going.

"Never liked it much," Gran replied. "Food is simply a means to an end. I eat to live. That's it. I suppose you're one of those foodies."

She made it sound like foodies were a scourge upon the earth.

"I like to eat," Kyle said with a grin, flipping the pieces of chicken in the pan. This was the last batch. The rest were covered in foil on a platter waiting to be served. "I think good food should be savored with good friends."

Dropping a stick of butter into the potatoes, Emmy coughed and choked slightly. I gave her a deadly look which had her ducking her head to hide her face. She couldn't fool me. She was laughing.

This wasn't even remotely funny.

"Ash, do you have any chicken broth?" Emmy asked, clearing her throat. "It will give the potatoes more flavor."

Casting a glance over at my grandmother, I nodded. "In the pantry. I'll get it."

My "pantry" was actually the closet in the foyer of my house. The kitchen was small, not many cabinets, so I'd had to take over any spare space that I could.

Rummaging through the shelves in the pantry, I reached all the way to the back for the can of chicken broth, but another longer arm beat me to it. Kyle plucked it from its spot and held it up triumphantly.

"Got it for you."

"Who's watching the chicken?"

And Gran.

"Shelby. Apparently Brad and George have hit it off and she thinks they might elope after dinner."

Giggling, I pulled Kyle behind the door so no one could see us. "It sounds like they have a five-alarm bromance."

"They do. I haven't seen George this animated since we came to Arborville. I think he misses his brothers. They're all way into sports trivia and trying to outdo the other." He quickly looked over his shoulder. "You seem tense, babe. We're supposed to be having a party."

"How can you be so calm?" I marveled. "Gran has been staring at you with hate-laser eyes since you got here."

Chuckling, he pulled me into his arms and brushed his lips against mine. "Parents never like the guy that's doing it with their little girl. A guy gets used to it. I'll win her over. You'll see. By the end of the evening, she'll love me."

"It?"

"You know…sex," he whispered in my ear, his breath warm on my cheek. "Parents are funny that way."

Great. Now I was thinking about us having sex. Why did I invite all these people over? And why didn't I ask Gran to stay at a hotel?

"She doesn't change her mind easily."

"Then let's say she won't love me, but she'll hate me less? How does that sound?"

Like the best I could ask for under the circumstances.

★ ★ ★

THE EVENING WAS a disaster.

It had been tense but going pretty well through the salads and entrees, but took a turn for the worst at dessert. Gran, who had been behaving up until then, brought up a presentation Kyle had made about a year ago regarding artificial intelligence and the possible uses of that technology. It was off to the races and everyone taking a side.

Shelby took Kyle's side but Brad took Gran's. George was, of course, on the side of his friend and business partner which put him at odds with his new best buddy Brad. Shelby and Brad were growling at each other and Emmy was trying to play peacemaker. Meanwhile, I could barely get a word in edgewise. The entire dinner table was in an uproar and this couldn't be good for anyone's digestion. Personally, I wanted to throw up. That's how sickening this all felt.

Kyle, who had been easygoing and charming all evening, had finally had enough. "I said that it might be possible in the future, Senator. I didn't say that I, personally, was working on it. But if I was, it wouldn't be anyone's business but mine."

He couldn't have said anything worse. Gran slapped her fork onto the plate, her lemon cake forgotten.

"You're arrogant."

"I'm not the one trying to make decisions for other people."

The tension in the room was thick and I didn't have a clue as to how to defuse the ticking time bomb that was getting close to zero. Did I clip the red wire or the green?

Shelby, bless her, quickly stood and grabbed a few plates. "Emmy and I will help with the clearing and dishes, Ash. Brad, why don't you tell them about your ideas for a honeymoon? They might be able to weigh in on a few of them. So far we can't decide on a destination."

I didn't hesitate to flee. Hey, I'm not proud of it and I should have stayed as the barrier between the two people I loved most, but I'd been battered and beaten down and I didn't have much left to give. They were going to have to act like adults for a few minutes.

Shelby and Emmy were on my heels, carrying plates and bowls into the kitchen. From this safe distance, I could hear Brad weighing out the virtues of a ski trip versus Tuscany. I could only hope that Gran and Kyle might find some common ground when it came to desirable geographic locations.

Emmy set the dishes on the counter and wiped her forehead. "Damn, that was a tension-filled meal. I think I need a Zantac."

Shelby flipped open the dishwasher. "We're all going to need one before the night is over, but in the meantime, we need to try and keep the conversation light and friendly. Only bring up subjects they can't argue about."

"Like cupcakes and puppies?" I asked, scraping the dishes. "Gran doesn't like frosting. I wanted to show her how wonderful Kyle is, but this hasn't worked how I planned. They're arguing about whether humans are going to become slaves to robots over the next hundred years."

Emmy sighed, a dishtowel on her hand. "I would imagine it's inevitable."

Shelby gave her an elbow in the ribs. "You're not helping."

"To be fair, I'm not really trying. The only thing that would help those two is to throw them in a cage with a hunk of raw meat and see who comes out alive."

I pressed my fingers to my temples. "That is my grandmother and boyfriend you're talking about."

"I know." Emmy patted my arm. "They don't like each other, hon. Like…at all. Do not get in between them. You'll end up sliced to ribbons."

I looked at Shelby for some kind of support. "Okay, Doctor. What's your advice? Do you agree with Emmy?"

"I definitely agree that you need to stay out of it. This isn't your battle to fight. Your grandmother came to dinner loaded for bear and Kyle was within her sights. She had her mind made up before she sat down at the table."

"This sucks," I groaned. "Big ones."

Something passed between Emmy and Shelby, an unspoken conversation that only they were privy to. It was only a few seconds but when it was done, Emmy had murmured an excuse and exited the kitchen, leaving me with Shelby.

"You know we love you, right?" Shelby asked, stacking plates into the dishwasher. "And we'd do anything for you. Even be brutally honest."

Whatever was about to happen I wasn't going to like. The tension that was already coursing through my veins ramped up a few notches.

"I know that, and I love you guys, too."

"You're like a sister to me, Ashlyn."

"You're like a sister to me as well."

This was going to be so bad. So very bad.

"So when I say this, I'm saying it with all the love in my heart."

Shit.

"That's good."

What else could I say?

Shelby straightened from her task and wiped her hands on a dishtowel. "Your grandmother is a nightmare."

What?

"Gran?"

Shelby nodded. "Yes, your grandmother. She's a menace to society and to you in particular. I know that she took you in and raised you, and I know that you love her, but she's in the living room right now trying to break you and Kyle up. For no discernible reason that I can see other than he's as smart and successful as she is and it pisses her off. Or maybe she just likes you alone and miserable. I don't know and frankly, I don't care about her motivations. I only care about you. She's toxic and you need to get her out of your life until she understands decent boundaries in a relationship."

Boundaries. Toxic. Relationship. All the words a psychologist might use. But they'd never come up against anyone like Senator Roslyn Caldwell. She needed her own chapter in their textbooks.

"She thinks she's protecting me," I replied in a half-hearted attempt to defend my grandmother. She was perfectly capable of fighting her own battles, but I felt like I should do it since she wasn't here. "She thinks I'm giving up what I believe in for Kyle."

"Are you?"

I'd given that question a great deal of thought.

"No," I answered. "I'm not. It would be one thing if the houses could be saved but they're too far gone."

"I'm not talking about the houses and I doubt your grandmother is either," Shelby said with a shake of her head. "I'm talking about your entire belief system. Your respect for the past. It's something I've always liked about you. I'd hate for you to lose that."

That was an even easier query.

"Kyle has that respect, too. Maybe not to the extent that I do, collecting and selling things, but it's there. He loves black and white movies, and vinyl, and history, and everything that fascinates me. He's about the future, that's true, but he has a healthy respect for the past."

It was one of the reasons I'd so easily fallen in love with him.

"So what about your grandmother?"

That wasn't so clear cut.

"She's my grandmother." I threw up my hands in frustration. What did people expect me to do? "She took me in when my mom died and she raised me. She made sacrifices for me."

"And she'll never let you forget that."

The silence between Shelby and I stretched out painfully. She was trying to help. I got that. But she simply didn't understand everything.

"That's not fair," I said quietly. "She'd already raised her daughter and she thought she was finally free to pursue her career. Then I came along. It wasn't easy for her."

"It wasn't easy for you, either," Shelby shot back. "You were a child. A little kid, Ash. You didn't ask to lose your mother."

"You're twisting it all. Gran never acted like she resented me. She was great. She took me everywhere and taught me so much. She's an amazing person, too. She's accomplished great things."

"I just want you to be happy."

"Gran will stay for a few days and then she'll go back to Washington. Everything will go back to normal like it always does. This is how it always is. A little chaos and then peace.

You've seen it yourself."

We all simply had to hold on for a few more days. Gran never stayed longer than that and it would be months before she'd return.

"I have seen that," Shelby conceded. "You have to admit, however, that there's a little more chaos this time."

"It will all be fine."

I was an optimist at heart, and I'd found that things did usually work out.

"What about the next time she comes?"

"That's a long way down the road and by then she'll realize how happy Kyle and I are. She was simply taken by surprise this time. Once she gets used to the idea, she'll love him as much as I do." Okay, that might be an exaggeration, but I was sure they could get along. "They might even find they have a lot in common."

Shelby nodded and loaded the last glass into the dishwasher. "I applaud your positive thinking. A few of my patients could take some lessons from you. In the meantime, though, we should probably get back out there. Someone has to play referee."

Lucky me.

CHAPTER TWENTY-FIVE

Ashlyn

WITH A SIGH of relief, I closed the front door. The last of the guests had left, including Kyle whom I'd barely had a chance to say goodnight to. We'd never had a chance to be alone all evening and since he'd given George a ride to dinner, I didn't get more than a quick peck of a kiss before he left. I'd make it up to him tomorrow. Right now, I had to talk to the woman who was currently pouring herself a glass of wine in the kitchen.

I marched in as Gran was re-corking the bottle. "You were very rude to Kyle."

We'd always had a strict honesty policy since I'd come to live with her all those years ago, so I didn't see any reason to hold back tonight.

"He was rude to me."

"He defended himself. He was trying to be nice but you kept going after him, Gran. What was he supposed to do?"

"I was simply seeing what the boy is made of. Looks like he has a thin skin, if you ask me."

Anger simmered in my gut, making dinner churn. "No one asked you."

Gran walked passed me into the living room and sat down on the couch, reaching for the remote.

"You used to value my opinion."

"Is that what this is about, Gran? I don't ask for your advice enough anymore? I'm a grown woman and I would think that would be expected."

Gran took a sip of her wine. "I'm trying to help you."

"The houses—"

"This is not about the houses," Gran cut in. "It was never about the houses. I can stand losing that fight, but I can't stand watching you run headlong into heartbreak. I want to save you from that. This is about so much more than whether those homes should be spared. It's about your compatibility with this man, Ashlyn. It's about understanding when love isn't enough."

I fell down into a nearby easy chair, not sure what my grandmother was talking about. "I don't know what you mean. Kyle and I are very compatible. I've never been happier or more comfortable with any other man."

"I felt the same way about your grandfather, Ashlyn Rose. I was in love and I was blind to our differences. I rushed into marriage with him and before I knew it had a child. Unfortunately, we weren't blessed with wedded bliss. We fought like cats and dogs. We were so different, he and I. I swear we couldn't agree on the color of the sky. In the end, I couldn't take it anymore. Then it started all over again with her. Dana married a man that was different as well. She was a morning person and he liked to sleep in. She wanted quiet evenings and he liked to party. They were complete opposites. And just like Jim and I, they fought all the time. If your father hadn't been sick, I'm sure they would have ended up divorcing, too. But the cycle in this family doesn't have to continue. I want to keep you from repeating our mistakes."

My grandmother should have been exhausted from the leap in logic she'd just taken.

"We just started dating and you have us married and divorced already."

"Start as you mean to go on."

Gran had said that to me since I was a child.

"You never told me this about my parents."

I didn't remember my father; he'd died when I was only two and then my mother had been killed in a car accident when I was ten. I did remember her. She laughed a lot and liked to dance around the kitchen. She liked to watch old movie musicals and she'd had a huge collection of dusty books that I used to page through long before I could read.

"You weren't old enough to hear about it and then it didn't seem important. It was so long ago."

From the look on my grandmother's face, however, it might have been yesterday. Her gaze was unfocused and far away, in another time and place. She was thinking about my mother. She always had that pained and lost expression when she did. My own heart squeezed hard in my chest at the feeling of loss we both felt so keenly. I'd lost a mother, but Gran had lost a child. I wasn't sure which was worse.

They both sucked, and our losses had molded us into the people we were now. For better or worse.

"I warned you when you were younger, but it seems I have to do it again," Gran went on. "I told you that you needed to find a man that had the same values and beliefs that you did. Otherwise, you're setting yourself up for disaster, Ashlyn."

"Kyle is a good person," I pressed. "I really love him, and I want you to give him a chance."

Gran took another sip of her wine and then set it on the side table. "I don't doubt that he's a fine person. I only question whether you two can make a good match. Lord knows that your mother and I were blinded by love."

"I'm not you or Mom. I'm me."

Smiling, she shook her head. "Young people always think that their situation is completely different and unique to any that came before it. This story, Ashlyn, is as old as time. Love is wonderful and fun, but it isn't always enough to keep a couple together for the long haul. All that I ask is that you slow down a little. Think about what you're doing and really take a look at what your future with Kyle Lewis would be like. Because tonight at dinner was just a taste of what you have to look forward to."

"Is that a threat?"

"No, it's a prediction. I was playing devil's advocate with your young man tonight but there are people all over this wide world that think that way. Do you think that you and he will somehow be insulated from those that will question him, his work? And you? You'll be pulled into it, too. Whether you believe in what he's doing, people will think you support it because you're with him. You'll be tarred with the same brush and it will affect you from business dealings to friendships to who your kids can play with at school. If you pursue this relationship, you might as well give up having any life or business of your own. He'll take it over. It's not his fault, he can't help it. He's bigger than life now."

Wow, Gran had put a hell of a lot of thought into this and come up with a bleak as hell future for me. Was Washington full of cynics?

Slaps forehead. Figuratively. Of course, it is. Duh.

"I understand where you're coming from on this." I did. I think. "But I think you're only focusing on the negative, not the positive."

She leaned forward, our gazes clashing. "Let me remind you of a moment in your life less than a week ago. Remember all the press when you walked with him before his speech? All the cameras and reporters? They were all trained on him. You were merely an accessory. A pretty girl on the arm of a rich and famous man. No one will ever ask your opinion or what you believe. That's how it will be. Is that what you want? I didn't raise you to be a cipher."

We both knew the answer to that question, but I wasn't as sure that the grim depiction was the actual truth. Kyle had never made me feel less than. As for the press, neither he nor I could control them. Gran ought to know that. She'd been dealing with them for years.

Gran stood and leaned down to kiss my forehead. "Don't answer me now. I just want you to think about it. That's all I ask. Will you do that for me?"

How could I say no?

"I will," I said, already feeling crappy about this entire crappy situation. "But I won't make any other promises."

"I'm not asking for anything else. You're a smart young woman. You'll know what to do when the time comes."

I hoped to hell she was right because right now I didn't have a fucking clue. I only knew that I loved Kyle more than anyone I'd ever known.

Was it true? Was love not enough?

★ ★ ★

Kyle

"THAT WOMAN IS a meat grinder," George growled as we drove away from Ashlyn's home. "No, wait. That's not right. She's one of those wood chippers. They take in a perfectly good and sturdy limb and reduce it to wood chips within seconds. How on earth did Ashlyn turn out so normal with a grandmother like that?"

That was an excellent question and I'd been asking it in my head all evening. From the first moment I'd walked in Ashlyn's front door tonight, her grandmother had been gunning for me. I kept checking myself in the mirror thinking I might have a bullseye drawn on the back of my sweater.

"I've had more challenging evenings, but I can't remember any lately," I replied with a grimace. "She's a tough old bird. I bet she gives them hell in Congress."

"I'm not worried about the other senators, the president, or even the press. I'm worried about you. She doesn't want you anywhere near her granddaughter. This wasn't about the houses. This was fucking personal."

At some point during dinner that same idea had popped into my brain as well. This was far more than a few historic homes on a street. This was about…something. I wasn't even sure it was truly about me. Roslyn Caldwell had a chip on her shoulder the size of a redwood. Maybe she hated inventors, maybe she hated coding and software, maybe she just didn't like guys with dark blond hair. I didn't know and I'm not sure it would have mattered anyway. She'd dug in her heels and she wasn't going to budge. Not anytime soon.

"According to Ashlyn, she only comes around for a few days a year. I'm not going to worry about what one woman thinks about me. It would be great if we got along but if we don't…"

I shrugged carelessly as if I didn't give a shit. I mostly didn't. As a lightning rod for controversy, I was used to people hating me for what I did for a living or what they thought I might do at some unspecified time in the future. I'd learned not to take too much to heart and let it go. Everyone simply wasn't going to like me. Full stop.

"Sure will make Thanksgiving awkward as hell," George said. "Come on, be honest. You don't want her to like you…just a little bit?"

The trouble with having a good friend like George is that he knew me so well. Dammit.

"Maybe a little," I conceded. "It would make life easier, especially for Ashlyn. I felt so sorry for her tonight, stuck in the middle."

George gave me a sideways look. "She means to make Ashlyn choose between the two of you."

No. Just…no.

"She wouldn't do that. She loves Ashlyn."

"I'm telling you that's what all this is about," George persisted. "I wish I was wrong, but I'm not. I saw the gleam in her eyes. I don't know what her motivation is but she's going to throw down the gauntlet, dude, and you better be ready for it. She absolutely meant to put Ashlyn in the middle and she's going to keep her there until she chooses one of you."

I was a tech guy and didn't always read people as well as George did. That's why we made such a good team. He could often see what was going on with others better than I could. I didn't want to believe what he was saying, though.

Because, frankly, it would be a shitty thing to do to someone you love. Making them choose. Who the fuck would do that?

"I don't think it's going to come to that," I finally said, realizing that I hadn't answered. I was too in my head tonight. "At least, let's hope it doesn't."

Ashlyn and I hadn't known each other long enough for me to be confident that in the end she'd choose me. I didn't want her to have to make a choice. As far as I was concerned, Roslyn and I needed to adult-up and try and get along. If only for Ashlyn's sake. If we couldn't we could just avoid each other. Families had been doing it for generations on holidays and other special occasions. I'm sure I could do it.

"Damn, you're an optimist. I'm telling you that woman isn't going to give up."

"Neither am I."

I'd stand by Ashlyn as long as she needed me to.

CHAPTER TWENTY-SIX

Kyle

DETERMINED TO HAVE some time with the woman I loved, I showed up at the retro store the next day around lunchtime. I had a plan and it entailed sweeping this beautiful female off of her feet. Neither of us had enjoyed the dinner party last night and we both deserved a meal that didn't need to be taken with massive amounts of antacid.

"Hey Katie, please tell me that Ashlyn is here."

The pretty assistant smiled and nodded toward the back room. "She is and buried in paperwork. Are you here to save her from being crushed by a mountain of dead trees?"

"I am. Can you watch the store while I whisk her away for a little while?"

"Absolutely."

Convincing Ashlyn, however, wasn't as easy.

"I can't just leave," she argued, her gaze sweeping across her desk. It wasn't as bad as I'd pictured, actually. "This is my store and my responsibility."

"I'm asking you to lunch, not on a two-week vacation. Katie said she could handle things while you were gone."

Heaving a loud sigh, Ashlyn stood from her chair. "Fine. I

am hungry."

This was strange. Weird. Not like the woman I knew. We were in the early stages of love, shouldn't we be wanting to spend all of our time together?

A frisson of awareness ran up my spine and an uneasy feeling took up residence in my gut. Something had changed in the last twelve hours and it wasn't me.

By the time we arrived at the barbecue joint we both loved, she'd barely looked me in the eye.

Although I wasn't always intuitive when it came to people and interpersonal relationships, I wasn't stupid, either. Ashlyn wasn't my first girlfriend and she sure as hell wasn't the first to sit stiffly across from me at the dinner table barely responding when I tried to start a conversation. She wasn't the first to stare off into space as if contemplating the universe, and she wasn't the first to dump me.

Because that's where this was headed. Ashlyn was going to kick me to the curb. Maybe not today, maybe not tomorrow, but soon.

George was right. The senator must have worked faster than I'd ever imagined.

It fucking hurt.

The waitress delivered our drinks and took our lunch order before disappearing back into the kitchen. We'd be on our own until she brought our meals. Time to get her attention.

"So I was thinking that I'd sell the company, my house, my car, and all my possessions and just head to Fiji. Give up wearing clothes. Work on my tan and my novel. Maybe develop a drinking problem."

Ashlyn frowned as if trying to make sense of my words and then shook her head. "What? I don't understand."

Of course not. I'd never been to Fiji and I was sure they made people wear clothes there.

"Are you with me now? Because you've been far away since I picked you up."

Her cheeks turned pink and she took a sip of her soda. "I have a lot on my mind. I told you that I'm very busy at work."

"You did," I conceded. "But you do have to eat. Is everything okay?"

She blinked once. Then twice. "Why wouldn't it be?"

"Because you're answering every question with a question."

That pink in her cheeks turned to a deeper red. "I didn't sleep well last night."

Now we were getting somewhere.

"Neither did I. It was an uncomfortable dinner. That was why I was determined for you and I to have some time together today. We didn't get it last night."

"No, we didn't." She fiddled with her fork, her gaze skittering away and then back. "I want to apologize for my grandmother last night. She should never have spoken to you that way. I talked to her about it after you left."

"You don't have to apologize for her. She's responsible for her own actions, not you. I'm sorry that you're in the middle of all of this, though." I reached out across the table and placed my hand on hers, entangling our fingers. "When your grandmother goes back to Washington, we'll make up for lost time."

I held my breath, waiting for her to tell me she had other plans and I wasn't in them.

Instead I received the first smile of the day. "We will."

Maybe I'd read the situation wrong. At this moment, she didn't look like a woman about to break my heart.

"In the meantime, I don't want you to worry about me and your grandmother. We'll be fine. I can deal with her while she's here."

"About that…"

She was shredding the corner of her paper napkin.

"Honey, you look like you have something on your mind."

Her chest rose and then fell as she took a deep breath. "I do, actually. I think it might be a good idea if you and I took a break while Gran is here. She won't be here much longer."

A break. Ashlyn wanted to take a break. It wasn't as bad as breaking it off but sure as fuck wasn't all that great, either.

Carefully, I controlled my expression, trying to appear neutral. Ashlyn was emotional enough for both of us. Tears had sprung to her eyes and one was already rolling down her cheek. Angus churned in my stomach and acid rose in the back of my throat. Senator Roslyn Caldwell had done this. She'd placed her granddaughter firmly in the middle. Cruel. The action was cruel and unnecessary.

"Don't put yourself through this, Ashlyn. Your grandmother and I will work this out eventually. Just let us do it. You don't have to place yourself between us."

She was already shaking her head in denial. "I think that I do. Gran isn't going to change her mind, Kyle."

"In time–"

"No," she interrupted. "She's not going to. Maybe eventually she'll get used to it, but she won't change her mind. That's not something she does very often. She thinks we're too different to make it…you know…for the long haul."

"She barely knows me. I'm more than what's been written or said about me. Half of it isn't even true."

That poor napkin was in pieces. It never stood a chance.

"It's a long story but trust me when I say that Gran has made up her mind. Honestly, I just want to keep the peace for the next few days. Can we–can we just take a little break?"

I couldn't say what I really wanted to. That her crazy grand-mother shouldn't be dictating our lives, but I also didn't want to be like Roslyn and place Ashlyn in the middle.

If I pushed back on this, I'd be doing that.

It went against every instinct I had and my heart was scream-ing bloody murder, but I nodded in agreement.

"As long as it's only for a few days."

"It will be," Ashlyn replied quickly, relief showing in every line of her body. Ten seconds ago she'd been so tense and now she was much more relaxed. At least I'd been able to do that. I loved her, dammit, of course I wanted to make her feel better. "She never stays too long, and she won't be back for months."

The first good news I'd had today.

I couldn't keep my mouth shut, however. "I'm not happy about this, Ashlyn."

Her mouth was turned down and another tear rolled down her cheek. "I know. I'm not either."

"Then why are we doing this again? You're a grown woman. You shouldn't have to bend yourself into a pretzel to make Roslyn Caldwell happy. She shouldn't have that kind of power over you. Or us."

Now she was tense again. Fan-fucking-tastic. I was the greatest boyfriend ever.

"She took me in when my mom died. She didn't have to, but she did. If it makes her feel better to think that I'm giving this relationship some thought—"

"Is that what she asked you to do?" I broke in, fresh anger making me hot under the collar. "She asked you to stay away from me?"

"She just asked me to think about things," Ashlyn said in what I assumed was supposed to be a soothing tone. Fuck that.

"And what did you say?"

I sounded pissed off but that was because I was, indeed, pissed the hell off.

"I said I would."

I was hurt. And angry. It was my only explanation for how I lashed out at that moment.

"Let me help you with that. If you're not all in, then maybe we shouldn't take a break. Maybe we should just end things. It would make life easier for you and your grandmother would get what she's been hoping for. Me out of the picture."

Her face turned pale and I could hear a quick indrawn breath. Bullseye. I'd just shoved a virtual knife in her heart. It matched the one she'd shoved in mine.

"I don't want to end things—"

"But you don't want Roslyn to know that we're together. You want her to think that you're mulling your options."

"Yes."

Ashlyn's voice was small and she was having a hard time looking at me. She was miserable but now so was I. I'd started this conversation feeling sorry for her but now I was mad.

"I think you need to do what your grandmother said and think about what you really want and whether I'm it. Right now, I'm not feeling like you're sure and if I'm going to keep putting myself out there I need to know that you're all in."

I'd made my girlfriend cry, tears rolling down her face. I handed her my own paper napkin and she hid behind it, not wanting the other diners to see her crying. Not a shining moment in my life, but then I'd never had my heart stomped on this badly. It made a guy do things he wouldn't normally do. I kind of wanted to cry, too. Or maybe slam my fist into a brick wall. Then the pain in my hand might be greater than the pain in my heart.

To me it seemed straightforward and simple. If Ashlyn loved me, she wouldn't care about her grandmother's opinion. End of story. It made me feel taken in and incredibly stupid.

"Are you breaking up with me?" she tearfully asked, her voice thick.

A lump had lodged in my own throat at her question. Was I? I didn't want to, but I also didn't want to get another sledgehammer to the chest.

"No."

"It sounds like you are."

"I'm not."

Because I loved her. I didn't want it to end.

"I love you."

"I love you, too."

Silence followed our declarations. It seemed we had run out of things to say. The waitress – with impeccable timing –

appeared and placed our meals in front of us. Now we didn't have to talk. It wasn't getting us anywhere and the entire conversation felt like we'd only run a few laps. No real progress.

Had we broken up? We were definitely on a break. Could I call her or text? We were in no man's land and now I didn't know what I was supposed to do or say. It reminded me of something my mom had once said to my older sister.

Sometimes love isn't enough.

I hoped it wasn't true this time.

CHAPTER TWENTY-SEVEN

Ashlyn

I WAS MISERABLE and it was my own fault.

I couldn't blame Kyle because he'd clearly been blindsided by my request for a break. I couldn't blame Gran because she couldn't technically make me do anything. This was all on me.

I'd thought I would feel better with some space from Kyle while Gran was here, but I only felt worse.

Like the gentleman that he was, Kyle offered to walk me back to the store, but I said that I had to make a stop on the way. That was total bullshit. I simply couldn't let him walk next to me for five city blocks in silence. I'd hurt him along with myself and I felt like the worst person alive.

Apparently, I didn't look all that well when I walked into the store. Katie's eyes went round and she immediately bundled me into the backroom, probably so I wouldn't scare the customers. At some point, she shoved a cup of tea in my hand and murmured words I wasn't listening to. I sat there sipping at the tasteless beverage and crying until Shelby showed up, Emmy right on her heels.

They fussed over me, wrapping me back into my coat and into the backseat of Shelby's vehicle with me too numb to object. I barely paid attention to where they were driving me but within minutes we were pulling into the garage of Shelby's home. I let them lead me into the house, take my coat, and pour me a whiskey.

It burned all the way down, but the slight pain finally woke me out of my stupor. That's when the tears started again. I was surprised I had any moisture left in my body.

"It's all my fault," I croaked after taking a second shot of the amber-colored liquor and feeling the fire all the way to my belly. "You shouldn't be nice to me. I'm a terrible person. I deserve this."

Shelby sat next to me on the couch while Emmy sat in the armchair. She'd brought out a bag of crackers and some cheese which made my stomach lurch. Whiskey didn't pair well with cheddar and the barbecue I'd barely eaten at the restaurant was already in danger of making a reappearance.

"Why don't you start at the beginning?" Shelby suggested, patting my hand. "We don't even know what's happened. We only know that Katie called us in a panic saying that you looked like a zombie and that you'd clearly been crying."

Emmy's eyes narrowed dangerously. "Tell us who made you cry and we'll kick 'em where it hurts. Male or female."

"Where does it hurt on a woman?" I asked, my brows pulled down. "I know where it hurts on a guy."

Shrugging, Emmy popped a piece of cheese into her mouth. "I would imagine it would hurt to get kicked in the tits."

"I don't think we need to go that far," Shelby said in that warning tone I'd heard so much. "Let's put kicking on the back burner. Ash, what's going on? Is it Kyle? Or your grandmother?"

Emmy sat up straight in her chair, her eyes wide. "Oh my God, did someone die?"

I needed to nip this in the bud immediately.

"No one is dead." I sniffled and Shelby handed me the box of tissues on the end table. "Kyle and I are...on a break."

Wrinkling her nose, Emmy fumed. "That sniveling little coward. He couldn't take a few more days of your grandmother? What a fucking weenie."

"I'm the weenie," I admitted with a groan, slapping my hands over my face in shame. "It was my idea."

Silence. Just...silence. Finally, Shelby spoke up.

"I think you need to walk us through it, Ash. Start at the very beginning. As in when you thought this was a good idea, and before you talked to Kyle."

Between sobs and a few more shots, I told them about my conversation with Gran and what she'd told me about my parents and then her marriage as well. I told them that I'd spent all night thinking about it and wondering whether she was right. Whether love was enough and all of that.

"Love isn't enough," Shelby said. "But it's a start if two people are willing to work at the relationship."

"So you decided to go on a break with Kyle?" Emmy prompted. "How did that come out of wondering whether love was enough?"

How could I even begin to explain what I barely understood myself?

"It was all so clear in my mind this morning," I replied, my mind drifting back to the decision I'd made in the shower. Usually the decisions made when wet were good ones. "I felt smothered by my grandmother and I needed space. I felt too much pressure and I just wanted it to end. I thought that if Kyle was out of the picture while Gran was here that the pressure would be off and I'd feel better."

Emmy and Shelby exchanged a quick glance and then Emmy leaned forward. "If it was your grandmother suffocating you then why didn't you take a break from her and not Kyle?"

I buried my face in my hands again. "Don't confuse me with logic. Honestly, I didn't think it was an option. You can't take a break from your family."

"Sure you can," Shelby said. "And sometimes you should. Like now, perhaps."

"You've never liked my grandmother."

"Now that's not true," Shelby said with a shake of her head. "I think your grandmother is a terrific senator. I think she has some issues in the grandma department, that's all."

"She raised me when she didn't have to."

"You keep saying that," Emmy replied. "As if she did you a huge favor. You were a child. Let me repeat that...a child. Of course, she took you in. You were her freakin' granddaughter and she was able-bodied. You would have done the same thing. We all would have. You're not her burden, you're her family."

"Your grandmother clearly has issues and now she's laid them all on you," Shelby said, censure in her tone. My friend was not happy. "I get that she had a bad marriage and then her daughter had one too, but that doesn't mean that you will. It's not a family curse, for heaven's sake. Seriously, she doesn't think your family has been cursed by voodoo, right? Because that would be weird...and unlikely."

"She talked about breaking the cycle, but I don't think she believes we're actually cursed. Gran is pretty cynical, so I doubt she believes in witches or magic."

"Then perhaps she's overreacting?" Emmy suggested. "People get divorced. People get unhappy in relationships. Sometimes people make it work."

"She thinks we're too different," I said. "She said it's a recipe for disaster. And no, Shelby, I haven't finished the book."

I'd already known what my friend was going to ask. I doubted Shelby had addressed a mess like this.

"I'm going to add a chapter just for this," Shelby declared. "When your family is batshit crazy and tries to interfere in your life. She's running a guilt trip on you, Ash."

"She's doing a great job of it. I promised her I'd think about my relationship with Kyle."

Emmy slapped a cracker down on the coffee table. "Shelby may like your grandmother but I don't think that I do. She should never have extracted that promise. It smacks of blackmail. She's guilted you all these years about taking you in and now all she wants you to do in return is break up with your boyfriend. Sure, that's fair."

Emmy's tone dripped sarcasm and Shelby shot her a warning look.

"What I think Emmy's trying to say is that your grandmother isn't the one that should be making these decisions in your life. You should be doing that."

"I know. Frankly, I don't know what comes over me when Gran is here. I'm usually a strong independent woman but the minute she comes into town I regress back to a little girl."

Shelby poured us all another shot. I was already feeling a little woozy, but I was going to drink it.

"Wanting a parent's approval is normal," she observed. "Not strange in the least. Now tell us about today. What happened with Kyle?"

What *had* happened? It was an hour of my life that had seemed to last for days. Almost in slow motion. A really terrible, awful day at quarter-speed.

"Kyle stopped by the store out of the blue to take me to lunch. I'd been avoiding him all morning because I'd wanted to put off the conversation about taking a break as long as possible," I explained. "But of course, I went to lunch with him. We went to the barbecue place down the street."

"And then?" Shelby prompted.

"We both ordered the brisket."

"You're delaying," Emmy said. "Spill it."

So I did. I told them all the dirty details. The crying, the sympathy – at first, and then the anger and silence while we ate.

"He was mad at you," Shelby said. "Were you mad at him?"

"A little," I admitted. "I kept thinking he could have been more understanding, but then I think that he was probably surprised and upset. He looked upset, anyway."

"How did that make you feel?"

I groaned and rolled my eyes at Shelby's question. She couldn't shake her training, not even now.

"Like a giant turd, thank you very much. I never wanted to hurt him. I just thought…"

"What…what did you think was going to happen?" Emmy asked incredulously. "You were going to chat over a dead cow and mutually decide to put your grandmother over your burgeoning relationship? And Kyle would be just okey dokey with it and you'd both leave the restaurant smiling, hand in hand? He'd go off and just wait in a holding pattern while you dealt with your family curse? Is that what you thought? Because that's even crazier than a voodoo spell."

When she said it like that…. It did make me sound completely delusional.

My head was really hurting now and that whiskey in my stomach was turning to pure acid.

"I did. I really thought it would be okay. I am such an idiot."

No one argued with me. They agreed.

"What do I do now?" My gaze ricocheted between my two friends. "How do I fix this? I messed up. I had a crazy moment. I'm better now. Shit, Kyle must hate me."

"I'm sure he doesn't hate you," Shelby said, eyeing the whiskey bottle. I was definitely done drinking for the day. I might already be drunk. "Just call him and tell him you had a moment of insanity and you made a mistake."

That sounded…doable. Kyle was a forgiving man. I hoped.

"What about Gran?"

"Tell her to butt out," Emmy said. "And to keep her neurosis to herself. We're all full here."

Shelby gave Emmy another look. "Some people find it easier to let their relatives talk and just nod as if you agree but then go and do whatever you want. It's your life, after all. They can give their opinion, but you don't have to take it. Technically you don't have to take ours, either."

"But you should," Emmy said quickly. "You really should."

I felt better. And sick to my stomach but I think it was from the booze, not the situation.

"I am going to take your advice. Right after I throw up."

Shelby and Emmy sprang to their feet and dragged me to the bathroom. I hadn't seen them move that fast in a long time.

They held my hair while I purged brisket and whiskey. Then they ran a cold washcloth over my face and told me it was all going to be alright. Kyle would understand because he was an amazing man.

I believed them, but then I was drunk.

CHAPTER TWENTY-EIGHT

Kyle

ALL THE WAY back to my house, I vacillated between anger and hurt, never quite settling on the correct emotion. I was pissed that Ashlyn would back away from us because her grandmother had issues. What those issues were I didn't know, but they clearly had shaped the older woman's decision-making when it came to her marriage and her daughter's. I was also hurt because I'd thought that we had something special, something...more.

I didn't like being in limbo, wondering where our relationship stood. In Florida it had all been so easy. We were the center of each other's world. Here at home it was far more complicated.

George's car was sitting in my driveway when I pulled into the garage. Working out of my house had its advantages but today it sucked. I wanted to drink a few beers and veg out in front of the television. George was going to wonder what the fuck was wrong with me and then he'd want to fucking talk about it.

There was a box of cupcakes on the kitchen counter when I walked in. Sam greeting me at the door, tail wagging. After some sloppy kisses I headed straight for the box. I wasn't the prom queen who had just been dumped by the captain of the football team but I was on those little cakes in a New York minute, shoving a mouthful of chocolate and buttercream into my mouth. Then I wouldn't have to talk.

George must have heard me because he wandered out of the office, giving Sam a pet before the canine retired to his spot on the cushion. I'd taken him on a long walk this morning and for all I knew George had done the same thing while I'd been gone. "I was going to tell you that I stopped at the bakery, but I see you already know. The lemon were for you and the chocolate for me but hey, whatever."

I took another huge bite out of the cupcake, crumbs dribbling down on my shirt. I didn't give a shit.

He eyed me from head to toe as I finished off the chocolate confection, wiping my fingers on my blue jeans. "Rough lunch?"

"What makes you say that?"

I reached for another cupcake. Lemon this time. I wasn't a complete jerk.

"Just a gut feeling. How are the cupcakes?"

"They're great," I said, my mouth stuffed full of lemon curd. "Fantastic."

"Good. That's good." George slid onto a barstool at the kitchen island. Here we go. "Anything you want to tell me?"

"Not particularly."

"Are you sure?"

"Absolutely sure."

"Okay, then I have news for you. If you want to hear it."

I finished the lemon and licked my fingers. "I'm listening."

"I hope so. I talked to the city council members and they've verbally agreed to let us move the campus to that large lot on the edge of town. It was our second choice. Lots of space and parking."

"But not many amenities nearby," I finished for him. "That's why it was second."

Not that any of this mattered anymore. I'd wanted to move the campus because of Ashlyn but now I wasn't even sure she was part of the equation.

"Right," George agreed. "The council said that they might be able to offer businesses some sort of incentives if they relocated closer so we wouldn't be so isolated out there."

I reached for another cupcake. I already wanted to puke so I might as well go all the way. George's brows shot up in surprise.

"Easy there," he cautioned, pushing the box of cupcakes away. He'd bought a dozen. I wondered how many I could eat before I threw up. All of them? Maybe. "Pace yourself."

"Fuck you."

"And there's your problem again."

"Okay, fuck you twice."

"I shouldn't tell you my other news, either. You don't deserve it."

"If you don't tell me, I'll fire you."

George just snorted at my threat as I assumed he would. I would never fire him and he knew it.

"You couldn't get through one day without me so go ahead and try it. You'd be begging me to come back before lunch." He reached into the box and pulled out his own cupcake. "Now do you want my other news?"

"I do."

"I received the engineering report today. With a bucketload of money and time, two of those houses can be saved."

This was the second surprise of the day, and under different circumstances, would have been terrific news.

"That's great."

"You look underwhelmed. I'd thought you'd be happy. In fact, I was so sure you would be happy I invited the head engineer here this afternoon to discuss what it would entail. I doubt the city council would be upset if we told them 'never mind' on that other lot. They're just thrilled we're going to build here."

"That's fine," I replied automatically, my mind still whirling with the news. I'd already made up my mind. If I could save even one of those houses I wanted to, whether I was with Ashlyn or not. "I'll take the meeting."

"I can do it–"

"No, it's fine. I'll do it."

"You might want to take some Pepto before she gets here. You look green."

I felt it, too. My stomach lurched dangerously as I ate the last bite of the cupcake. How many was that?

"I've felt better. I think I just need to lie down for a few minutes."

"You need to lie down in the middle of the day?" George asked. "That's…different. Are you coming down with some-thing? Because if you are–"

George was a huge germaphobe.

"I'm not. I shouldn't have eaten those cupcakes so quickly."

"I have to agree with that. Now do you want to tell me why I found you shoving chocolate ganache into your piehole?"

"We covered this earlier. No, I don't."

George shrugged carelessly. "It can only be one thing. Ashlyn. So just turn right around and go back and apologize for whatever bonehead shit you did."

"What makes you think it was me? Maybe it was her."

"It was you."

I'd had enough today and it wasn't even two fucking o'clock in the fucking afternoon.

"It wasn't me," I replied hotly. "She's the one—"

I broke off when I realized I was about to say it out loud. Would that make it more real?

"*She's the one* that what? What did Ashlyn do?"

George was going to find out anyway. If not now, eventually.

"She wants to take a break while her grandmother is in town."

George digested the information for a moment and then nodded. "Sounds like a good plan. It should make her life a lot easier."

Shit, even my best friend had turned against me.

"I take it you don't agree?" he asked, taking a bite from the chocolate cupcake. "What do you think she should do?"

Anything other than this.

I threw up my hands, suddenly glad to be able to let all my anger out. "She just sprung it on me. No warning. Nothing. Just...I think we should take a break while my grandmother is here. What the fuck is that about?"

"I'm guessing it's about keeping her sanity. The senator is a real piece of work. Can you imagine living with that woman for years on end? She would have made me crazy within a month. Ashlyn should be making rag rugs with blunt scissors in a padded room. The fact that she's a functioning member of society says a hell of a lot about her strength."

"Strength? She folded to her grandmother's wishes. Roslyn Caldwell wants Ashlyn to think about our relationship."

"And you don't want her to do that? That sounds a little insecure, dude."

"I'm not insecure."

"You *sound* insecure."

"You sound like an asshole."

"There's that language again," George chuckled. "You're so predictable. Listen, try and see this from Ashlyn's point of view."

Turning, I grabbed two beers from the refrigerator, handing one to George. "I do see it from her perspective. I get that she's grateful to Roslyn for taking her in and all of that. I get that she doesn't want to rock the boat for the next few days. I get it, alright? But still…"

George winced when I took a swig of my beer. "Can I recommend something to you? Cupcakes and beer are a lousy combination. You'll make yourself sick. Personally, I would find that funny as hell, but you might not enjoy it as much."

My friend had a point. The taste combination was vile.

"Just fucking fantastic. Now I can't even enjoy a beer."

George stood and put the beers back into the fridge and then poured me a glass of water. "Drink this. It might make you feel better. Now what the hell is going on with you? She asked you to take a break and you lost your shit? Is that what I'm hearing?"

"I was mad," I admitted, taking a gulp of the water. It did

taste good after all that sugar. "Upset that she was giving in so easily to her grandmother."

"You don't know if it was easy."

"It felt like it."

"I still maintain that you don't know. So go on. She asked you to take a break while the senator is here?"

"She said it would only be for a few days, but I assured her that I could handle her grandmother. I've had worse."

"That's true. Lots of people hate your guts," George replied cheerfully. "You get death threats on a weekly basis."

"You don't have to sound so happy about it."

"Just making an observation. Touchy, aren't we? So you got mad and stomped out of the place? Is that about right?"

"It is not," I said succinctly. "I tried to control my temper, but I certainly did let her know that I wasn't happy about this. We ate our meal. I picked up the check and then offered to walk her back to her store. She said she had a stop to make on the way so I should head on back home. Personally, I think she was only making an excuse but what do I know? I'm a brain-dead idiot with a genius IQ."

"So call her and make nice. And for the love of Pete, stop stuffing your face with buttercream. It's not a manly look, dude."

"I can't call her."

Rubbing his face, George sighed. "Why not?"

"Because I think we might have broken up at lunch. I'm not sure."

"You're not sure," he repeated. "But you might have? Don't you think you'd know?"

"Normally I would but this was like an out of body experience."

"My parents begged me to go to med school," George said to no one in particular, not even looking at me. "Don't work for the genius, they said. He'll be weird, they said. Work at a regular company for a regular guy. I could have taken their advice, but no, I knew better. I wanted excitement and adventure."

"You got that."

George butted the heel of his hand against my forehead. "What in the fuck is wrong with you? Okay, listen up because I'm only going to say this once. I know that you have issues with interpersonal relationships and all that crap, but this is really common sense, my friend. You and Ashlyn haven't been together all that long. You are a new couple. Did you hear that part? Because it's important. You and she barely know each other and don't bother interrupting me and telling me how much you love each other. That's fantastic. Everyone loves a lover, right? But you haven't known one another for years. Her grandmother, however, has been in Ashlyn's life since she was a little girl. And whether we like it or not, our families have power over us. When I go home I let my mom do my laundry, for fuck's sake. She even butters my toast. I'm perfectly capable but I go back to being a little kid and for a few days I love it. I couldn't do it all the time, but it's okay for a weekend."

"What is your point?" I growled, already tired of being lectured to. "Get to it."

"I will." George pointed at me, his finger digging into my chest. "If Ashlyn needed you to hang back and stay out of sight for a few days then you should have been happy to do it. She asked you for a few days, not a few months or years. A few days. Shit, I've seen you disappear into the lab for a week at a time only surfacing when you couldn't stand the smell of yourself. So what she was asking you to do really wasn't a big deal. As for giving into her grandmother...of course she did. She might be a grown woman but that's her family. She's going to err on that side for awhile. Not forever hopefully, but for a time. You would have done the same thing for your parents and you know it."

"They would never ask that of me."

"That's not the point. The point is that you need to cut that poor girl some slack. She's like a chew toy in a tug of war between two mean dogs. You got your feelings hurt. Get the hell over it. Pick up your phone and call her. Work it out. You won't be happy until you do."

George had made a good argument and I couldn't fight it. I had been butthurt and I had let it cloud my logic. Roslyn had to be putting tremendous pressure on Ashlyn. I should have been more understanding and patient.

"I'll call her now."

"Call her in an hour." George nodded toward the front window where we could see a car parking in front of the house. From a sound sleep, Sam's ears perked up. "That engineer is here to talk about the houses. If you're still interested in saving them, that is."

I was. Even if Ashlyn didn't want me. But I hoped she still did. Want both of us, that is.

CHAPTER TWENTY-NINE

Ashlyn

AFTER ALL OF that whiskey I wasn't in any shape to drive, but then neither were my friends. They'd drank as much as I did. We waited a few hours and also ate some cheese and crackers. It wasn't too bad on my now pissed-off stomach and I did feel somewhat better, although not a hundred percent.

I wanted to head straight to Kyle's house, but Katie had a dentist appointment and I'd promised her the time off, so Shelby drove me back to the store. Katie was thrilled to see me in better shape than when I had left.

"I can stay here with you," Shelby said, her gaze running from my toes to the top of my head. "You know…keep you company."

"You don't have to do that. Don't you have classes to teach or something?"

Shelby had a private practice, but she also taught a few classes at the local junior college.

"I cancelled them for the day. I can stay here if you want me to."

I did want her to.

"That would be great, although I should probably work on

all that paperwork."

Wrinkling her nose in distaste, Shelby shook her head. "It can wait one more day. What you need to do is relax a little. Do you have any games in this store?"

Did I? What a silly question.

"Have you ever played Mousetrap?"

Shelby's eyes lit up. "It's one of my favorites."

"I'll set up the board."

"I'll grab us a couple of ginger ales from the back," Shelby said. "It will settle your stomach."

It was a plan. I was beginning to feel like an actual human being again.

Shelby beat me three games out of five, but then that was our Shelby. She liked to win and she did it often. I didn't mind. I really just wanted the company. After the games, she helped me dust some shelves and reorganize the vinyl albums.

At one point, I thought about sending Kyle a text but that wasn't my style at all. I wanted to talk to him face to face. It was the old-fashioned part of me, I guess. I wanted to see his face when we talked and a text message with absolutely no nuance wasn't going to do it.

"What will you say to Kyle when you see him?"

Shelby was now helping me organize the toy shelves. She'd even waited on a customer. She might have missed her calling.

"First I'll say that I'm sorry. I handled the entire situation badly. Then I'll tell him I want our relationship to work. I just need a little space to deal with Gran."

"And how do you intend to deal with your grandmother?"

"I don't know," I admitted, stacking a Slinky on the shelf. "I just know that I have to stop caring about what Gran thinks. I have to stop letting her…what is it you and Emmy said? Fly in and shit all over my life and then fly out. She can't do that anymore."

"That's a big step," Shelby said quietly. "It won't be easy and Roslyn isn't going to give in quietly. She's going to fight to keep the status quo."

I was going to fight, too.

"I'll deal with it. With her. I love her, but she doesn't get to control my love life. She doesn't get to control my life at all, as a matter of fact." I took a deep breath. "The fact is I should probably talk to her before I speak with Kyle. I need him to know that I took some action. Otherwise, it's just words and they don't mean much."

"Our little girl is becoming a woman," Shelby sighed.

"It's far past time."

"Yes, but one of the things that makes you special is your tender heart, Ash. You desperately want everyone to be happy and you want to believe in fairy tales and happily ever-afters. We love that about you. It's only unhealthy when you let people take advantage of that. Like your gran. It's only natural to want to make our families happy, so don't beat yourself up about this."

"I hurt Kyle."

"Yes, and you probably will again. He'll do it, too. It's part of being in a relationship. Hopefully you learn and grow, do it less. But it's going to happen. It's how you deal with it that's important."

"Communication?" I guessed. That was Shelby's favorite word.

"You bet." She grinned and held up an old train engine. "And if you can't make it work with Kyle, we can all hop a train to nowhere. See the world. Or something like that. He adores you. It's as plain as the nose on my face. It's all going to be fine."

"You didn't see him today."

"I didn't have to. I've seen this in my practice and I can assure you that this all comes down to communication. You just need to talk and really listen to one another. You took him by surprise at lunch, but he'll have had time to digest it all by now. He'll see that you weren't trying to end things, you were just trying to get some space."

Speaking of digestion...I would never drink whiskey again. Ever. Next time I'd drown my sorrows in a chocolate milkshake. Extra whipped cream and sprinkles.

"I hope you're right. We were both pretty upset at the end of lunch."

"Have some faith. Normally you're the most optimistic person I know."

"My optimism is a little battered today, but I'll try. Any advice when I talk to Gran?"

Shelby nodded. "Be honest. Be calm. Be firm. Don't give into emotional pleas and for heaven's sake don't let her make you feel guilty."

"See? I don't need your book. I have you. But just for fun, what would your book have said?"

"That exact statement."

"I should have read it."

"Yes, you should have. There's still time."

First, I had to talk to Gran, and then I had to make up with

Kyle.

This wasn't going to be easy or pleasant. But it would be worth it. I was finally seeing the forest *and* the trees. Gran had issues…but they didn't have to be my issues.

★ ★ ★

Kyle

"CAN YOU WATCH Sam for me?"

I threw a pair of jeans and a couple of shirts into the suitcase open on my bed. Sam was sniffing at the luggage and pawing at it every now and then. He had to be realizing that something was up. I reached out and ruffled his fur and got a wet lick on the cheek in return. He'd be fine with George for a couple of days.

I was catching a flight out of O'Hare tonight heading for Seattle. My little sister was in labor and I was determined to see the newest addition to our ever-growing family in person. And that meant that this situation with Ashlyn was going to have to wait. I'd deal with it when I returned. It might give Roslyn Caldwell a chance to leave town.

Or turn her granddaughter completely against me. It could go either way.

"I will. Are you going to let Ashlyn know you're leaving town for a few days?"

I'd thought about it and I was tempted. But…

"If we're on a break, I doubt she'll notice I'm gone. She asked for a little time and this will make it much easier for me to give it to her. If I were in town I doubt I'd be able to stay away. Kathy going into labor might just be a blessing in disguise."

"I've always wondered about that saying. If I were a blessing I wouldn't wear a disguise."

I tossed in my shaving kit and an extra sweatshirt. "You want to talk philosophy? You just want to divert my attention from telling you not to feed Sam pizza."

"It was only the cheese."

"Do not feed my dog pizza. Or cheeseburgers. Or anything that comes in Styrofoam. He has food and treats. Tons of them. Please use those."

Sam's ears perked up. He knew the word *treat*.

"See? He thinks he's going to get a treat."

And now I'd said it twice.

"I'll get him one," George offered. "You're a real hard ass about cheese. Dogs love cheese and hamburger."

My friend disappeared for a moment and then came back with a *handful* of dog treats. I'd better not stay in Seattle very long or I'd come back to a dog that waddled.

"Go easy on those. That bag is supposed to be a month's supply."

"They're small."

"So is he. Don't feed him like a grown man."

"I won't. I promise. It's just that he's so cute when he begs."

"You're going to need to learn to turn down those big brown eyes."

"So you're not going to call her? Or send a text?"

I closed and zipped my bag shut. "I said no. She asked for space. I may not have been happy about giving it to her, but I did agree to do it. I won't go back on that."

"Maybe she doesn't really want it."

"Maybe she does." I was getting irritated, but it wasn't really George's fault. I was predisposed to be unhappy. "Listen, when I get back I'll call her. I'll be gone forty-eight hours. Tops. Unless of course Kathy takes days to deliver this baby. In the meantime, you have your assignment. Find me the best firm in the world to restore those homes. We're not moving the campus after all."

It didn't matter whether Ashlyn and I were together. They did have historic value to Arborville and if this town was going to be my new home, it seemed like the right thing to do to save them. My hope was to incorporate them in some way to the campus, but I'd leave that to the experts.

"The town council is going to be surprised."

"Everyone will but that's the fun part. Hopefully they'll think it's a good surprise and not a bad one. Either way they get the jobs they wanted."

"And Ashlyn gets to keep her houses."

"This isn't about her. This is about the community."

"It's going to cost more," George said in a warning tone. "A lot more. And it's going to take longer. We won't break ground this spring."

"But look what we'll have achieved when it's done. Like I've always said, let's do the hard things. The things no one else wants to do. That's what you'll look back on and be proud of. Those will be the accomplishments they'll talk about after we're gone."

"I doubt they'll talk about me when I'm gone. They may talk about you, though. Mostly they'll say you're a pain in the ass."

"Back at you, buddy."

I could hear the sound of car horn from outside. "The limo

is here to take me to the airport. You know what you need to do, right?"

"Don't feed the dog junk food and make a historic monument out of two homes. Sound good?"

"Perfect. I'll text you when I get to Seattle."

"A hundred bucks says it's another girl. You Lewises don't make boys in this generation."

So far, all the grandchildren had turned out to be female.

"I'll take that action. We're due for a boy."

George grinned and waggled his eyebrows. "This will be the easiest money I've made. Have a safe flight and I'll see you in a couple of days."

Would Ashlyn even know I'd been gone? Would she miss me?

I was going to miss her.

CHAPTER THIRTY

Ashlyn

W HEN I GOT home after the long, awful day Gran was sitting in the living room and talking on the phone. My heart pounding, I walked past her and into the kitchen to grab a water. I was parched and re-hydrating was a priority. Speaking to Gran was also a priority but it wasn't going to be easy.

Despite our vow to be honest with one another, it wasn't our way to bring sticky issues out into the open. We were more of a *sweep them under the rug* kind of family. Ignore it all and it would go away. But I'd come to realize that the issues didn't go away. They were always there just waiting to rear their ugly little heads.

Like today.

After a long pep talk from Shelby I was as ready as I would ever be to deal with my grandmother.

I settled onto a chair across from Gran and waited for her call to be over. After a few minutes, she hung up.

"You look like hell. Are you sick?"

"I've been better." I took a deep fortifying breath. Into the breech. Just do it. "Gran, I think it's time for you to go back to Washington."

There. I said it. The world hadn't crumbled into dust either.

"I'm still working on organizing the rally."

I shook my head and kept my voice firm and level. "There isn't going to be a rally. You're going to let this issue go and so am I."

Gran didn't get upset, which I think I would have preferred. Instead she studied me intently as if I was a creature she'd never seen before. In a way, I suppose I was. I was a new me.

"We don't have to give up. We can win this."

"I'm not giving up. If Kyle thought the houses could be saved, he would do that. There's no question. If they can't then we're only spinning our wheels. It's time to let this go." I paused for a moment and then rushed in. Like a fool. "Are you here for me, Gran, or for your career?"

"I came here to help my granddaughter, although now I'm beginning to wonder why. Your ingratitude is stunning."

Gratitude. That was a whole subject right there.

"I'm supposed to be grateful? For you taking me in after Mom died. For everything. The funny thing is, Gran, that I am grateful. But that doesn't mean you get to come in to town a couple of times a year and make a mess out of my life. It can't work like that any longer."

"A mess?" Gran sounded outraged and red was beginning to show in her cheeks. "I've done everything in my power to make sure that your life is wonderful, Ashlyn Rose. Who encouraged you to go into business for yourself when you didn't have the confidence?"

"You," I answered promptly. "I'm not saying that you're a terrible person, Gran. You're wonderful. Most of the time. But sometimes you've allowed your own issues to cloud your judgment."

"This is about Kyle Lewis."

"It's about a lot more than Kyle. This is about your issues with Granddad. And Mom. I don't know what happened–"

Gran stood and turned her back to me, staring out the window. "Stop right there. All I've been saying to you is that you need to think about what you're doing. Women always think they need a man, but they really don't. They just mess everything up and keep you from doing what you want to do. Then you end up not being the person you wanted to be. It may have happened to your mother, but I won't let it happen to you. When I took you in I promised myself that you'd have everything. Everything, Ashlyn. And I meant it."

She truly believed what she was saying. I could hear it in her voice.

"I have more than I ever believed was possible."

Gran turned and I could see her eyes shining with tears. I couldn't remember the last time – or if ever – I'd seen her even close to crying.

"Everything. You should have everything."

I shook my head. "No one should have everything. They'd be spoiled and they wouldn't have the space anyway. I have so much and you're the reason for a lot of it. My solid upbringing, for one thing. And you instilled a strong work ethic in me. Made sure that I valued education and helping my community and the world at large. You made me care about others because I saw how tirelessly you worked for the underdog, first in your law practice and then in the government. You were the example that

I looked to so many times in my life. But I'm not you, Gran. I'm not Mom, either. Your choices aren't mine. I'll say it again. I don't know what happened to you with Granddad and I don't know what happened to Mom with my dad, but I am a different person. I'm living my own life. Can't you see that?"

"Your mother wouldn't listen, either. I warned her that she was giving it all up to marry your father."

"Kyle and I aren't even close to getting married. But I don't think I'd be giving anything up. Yes, he's famous and I don't want to be. I don't want the spotlight. He's welcome to it and if I'm just the girl on his arm, that's fine with me. Let me ask you this, Gran, what is it that you want for me? What do you think I should be doing with my life?"

From the expression on Gran's face I wasn't going to like the answer.

"More."

"More," I echoed. "You want me to do more."

A stab to my heart. My grandmother wasn't as proud of me as I'd thought. Ouch.

"You can be so much more. You're a local business owner, Ashlyn. You could parlay that into running for town council, and then maybe the state legislature. Then later run for senator when I'm ready to retire. I could turn my entire political operation over to you. But you have to dedicate yourself to it, and a man will just get in the way."

"Is that what you did? Dedicate yourself?"

Gran nodded. "I did. I wanted to run for local office, but your grandfather discouraged me. Said that we had a young child and that I needed to be home more. He wanted me to have more children."

It was so clear now. She'd never told me these details before. Ever. But then what would I have done with them?

"You wanted Mom to follow in your footsteps, too?"

Gran threw up her hands in frustration. "I tried telling her that he was no good, but she was in love. She couldn't be swayed and she ran off with him. They were miserable practically from the beginning and then she got pregnant with you. It all went downhill from there. He ruined her life."

Because of me.

"So you decided that I would have the life you'd hoped for?"

"You could have more if you wanted it."

"This is so messed up. So you took me in and raised me to be...you?"

"Not at all. I simply wanted you to have all the options that I didn't. I wanted you to have choices, Ashlyn. Is that such a crime?"

No, it wasn't. It was actually kind of nice and sweet. Two words I'd never thought to describe Gran.

"It isn't a crime. But it's annoying when you're still pushing your choices down my throat when I've already made mine. I've made my choices, Gran, and I'm really pretty darn happy about them. I have a great life, with wonderful friends, and a terrific store. I even have a grandmother who makes journalists shake in their shoes. I'm good. Really."

She smiled then and chuckled. "I do that, don't I? They're terrified of me. It's so fun."

"And you help people," I went on. "People that really need you. I think maybe you've lost sight of that part lately."

"I just don't want you to have any regrets. Your grandfather and I fought like cats and dogs because we didn't see the world the same way. That's how it was with your parents, too. I want to save you from that."

I wondered if I would be the same with my children, wanting to save them from their questionable decisions. Probably. Some lessons, however, had to be learned the old-fashioned way. Firsthand.

"I'm afraid I can't let you do that, Gran. If I was jumping off a cliff, yes, please stop me. If I'm falling in love, you have to let me do it. Especially if the guy isn't a felon or a bad person in general. I think you and Kyle actually have a lot in common."

Gran walked up to me and placed her hands on my shoulders. She looked much older in that moment than I'd ever seen her, every line of worry on her face. "When I saw you together I was so scared for you. He's bigger than life, Ashlyn. He'll completely eclipse you."

"I'm okay with that." I placed my own hands on hers and gave them a squeeze. "I don't want the spotlight. I never have. But if I ever do want it, I guarantee you that he wouldn't stand in my way. Would it make you feel better if I asked him that?"

"It would make me feel better if he signed a paper and we had it notarized."

"I'll see what I can do about that. Now are we okay? Can you give me the space to make my own decisions even if you don't like them?"

For a moment I thought she was going to say no but them she nodded. "I can but it won't be easy."

Honesty. That's what I loved about Gran.

"We'll work on it together. I'm going to start now. There's something I need to tell you, Gran. Something I should have a long time ago."

She looked a little scared but lifted her chin as if to take the punch. "Just tell me."

"I hate those drapes."

"What?"

I pointed to the living room curtains. "I hate those drapes. You overruled my choice and pushed me into picking these. They're ugly. I hate flowers. I wanted the stripes."

Turning to study the hated draperies, she shook her head. "Well, you're wrong but on your own head be it. Flowers are better, but this is your house."

"That's progress, Gran. I'm proud of you."

We had a long way to go, but it was a start. Now I needed to see Kyle.

CHAPTER THIRTY-ONE

Ashlyn

I DROVE AS fast as the law allowed to Kyle's house, happy to still see lights on despite the later hour. There was so much I wanted to say to him but mostly I wanted to tell him that I loved him. Although new, our relationship was important. I wouldn't run again when it wasn't smooth sailing. I'd stick around and we'd face it. Together.

I could hear Sam barking when I rang the doorbell and my heart skipped a beat in my chest as the door swung open, only to plunge to my feet when I saw that it wasn't Kyle but George. As the designated best friend, he had to know what was going on between Kyle and I, but he didn't look shocked to see me there.

"Kyle's not here but you're welcome to come in. Sam and I ordered pizza and I'm not allowed to give the poor guy any of it. Do you like extra cheese?"

I hadn't come to eat but suddenly my stomach growled, reminding me that I'd had a rough day...digestively speaking. Maybe I could hang out and wait for Kyle to come back. Perhaps he had gone out for a late-night run. It was freezing outside but he didn't seem to mind the cold all that much.

"Your stomach answered for you," George said, stepping

back as I gave Sam a scratch behind the ears. "Come on in. It's cold as hell out there."

"Nothing like a prairie wind," I replied, shrugging off my heavy coat and scarf. The smells wafting from the kitchen were making my mouth water. "I could eat a little. Will Kyle be back soon?"

George retrieved a plate from a cabinet near the sink. "I don't think so. He went to see his sister Kathy. She's in labor. Did he mention that she was pregnant?"

He had, although it had been a brief mention as we'd talked about our families. I'd had no idea she was this close to actually having the baby.

I was also kind of hurt that he hadn't told me he was leaving town but then I reminded myself that it was my idea to be on a break. He was only following the rules.

"He did." I settled at the island, Sam right next to my knee hoping for a dropped piece of sausage or cheese. "But if he mentioned where she lived, I don't remember."

"Seattle," George said around a mouthful of pizza. "He flew out tonight. He said he'd be back in a few days barring any issues with Kathy. I assume you're here to talk with him about this *break* that you're on?"

So George did know about it. I wasn't surprised but I was embarrassed, the heat rising in my cheeks. He had to think I was the dumbest person on the planet, not being able to deal with my grandmother.

"I guess he told you about it."

I didn't know what else to say.

"I told him to text you that he was going out of town, but he said that he couldn't because you were both on a break."

His tone told me all I needed to know about his opinion of said *break*.

"I handled this badly."

"That's kind of an understatement." George took another big bite. "How's your grandmother?"

"Fine. She's leaving for Washington tonight. She's canceling the rally."

"What about the houses?"

"I understand that they can't be saved. It's sad but that's the way it is."

"You know Kyle has an engineering firm looking into that."

"I do and maybe they'll have good news, but I'm not going to count on that."

He nodded and reached for another slice. I was thinking that maybe I needed to stop at one and see how it sat in my tummy.

"That's very wise. Hope for the best but expect the worse. That's what my mom used to say."

"Gran said something like that, too."

"Your grandmother is...quite a woman."

"Is that your polite way of saying she's a piece of work?"

George grinned and took a draw from his beer while Sam leaned even closer to me, looking up with his big brown eyes. The pleading, the begging. I didn't know how Kyle kept from feeding this cute puppy a juicy steak every single day.

"That's one way of putting it. She's made a hell of a lot of noise and made Kyle's public relations firm earn their money this week."

"She means well. She's passionate about helping people. It's not all about getting re-elected. She really does want to do her best. I think she just got a little lost."

"I'm not questioning what she's done for her constituents. I'm only concerned with what she's doing to my friend. And you, too. I'd like to think that we're becoming friends."

He said it with such a gentle smile. Kyle had good taste in people.

Well...he had chosen me, after all.

"I'd like to think that, too. I'd never hurt Kyle on purpose. I want you to know that."

George's smile was replaced with a far more serious expression. "I'm glad to hear that. You have to understand him, Ashlyn. He's laser-focused when he's going after what he wants and that's why he's been successful. He's willing to do the work and put in the time. He does whatever it takes and he's goddamn brilliant. A freaking genius. Watching him work...it's amazing. But that's how he approaches relationships, too. If he believes in it, he throws himself in. All in. And I'll be honest with you. I've never seen him this in before. Ever. You're his person, and for him, that's it. Just like Kyle is Sam's person. You have the power to make him incredibly happy or break his heart. It's your choice what you do."

My throat had tightened listening to how Kyle loved me. I loved him that way too, but I hadn't been showing it.

"I won't break his heart. I came over here to tell him that. I'm all in, George."

"I'm glad to hear that. Now why don't you go home and pack a bag?"

I wasn't sure I understood what he was telling me.

"A bag? What for?"

"To fly to Seattle, of course."

Of course. Because I was Kyle's person and he was mine.

★ ★ ★

Kyle

IT WAS A girl. I'd lost a hundred bucks to George, but my sister Kathy and her husband Jesse now had the most beautiful little girl I'd ever seen. I'd sprinted into the hospital just as she was beginning to push. I'd done the hospital-uncle thing often enough now to know what that meant. A baby was imminent and sure enough less than an hour later Paige Marie had arrived with a mop of dark hair on her head and the tiniest bow for a mouth.

There wasn't a dry eye in the place, both sides of the family tearing up at the sight of the newest addition. I wasn't immune and I choked up when Jesse put baby Paige into my arms. Wrapped in a pink-striped blanket, she hardly weighed anything and had fallen asleep from her exhausting first night out into the world.

My heart was far too large for my chest and I could feel every single beat against my ribcage.

This. Right here.

My relationship with Ashlyn was fragile and new but I could see the two of us together – in a few years – getting married and having a baby. Maybe even a boy. He would have my hair and chin and Ashlyn's beautiful blue eyes. He'd learn kindness and a respect for the past from his mother, and he'd have a zest for the future from me. He'd be the best of both of us.

We had a hell of a lot of work to do before any of that would happen, but we had to be together to do it. We had so many firsts to look forward to if Ashlyn would only see how good we could be. I sure as hell had never thought about getting married or having a baby until I'd met this woman. She'd changed everything for me. One day I was an unashamed workaholic, the next I'm planning a future. No one was more shocked than I was.

As soon as I returned home I was going to see Ashlyn. Fuck this break. I needed to convince her that we could make this work. It wouldn't be easy, but I was ready to do the work if she was, too.

Mom and baby were tired and Jesse was as well, although he seemed to be high on adrenaline and black coffee. He might not sleep for days or he might crash the minute we left the hospital room. With a promise to come back in the morning after grabbing a few hours of sleep we one by one drifted away.

I wasn't the last to go. My parents had that distinction, but the sun was coming up when it was my time to leave. There was a large window at the end of the hallway between two elevator banks and from there I could see the orange and pink sky growing brighter with each passing minute. By the time I checked into my hotel it would be sunny outside, or as sunny as Seattle could be this time of year. I'd grab some breakfast and then hit the sack. My eyes felt gritty and my back was tight from sitting on the plane and then in an ergonomically nightmarish plastic chair in the waiting room. A hot shower would help and then later I might send Ashlyn a text. Just a hello and ask how she was doing. Nothing major. Just to touch base.

I missed her already.

The elevator doors slid open and I had to blink several times because I was sure I was hallucinating. The women standing there looked so much like Ashlyn. But she couldn't be. Because I was in Seattle and she was back in Arborville. I was so tired I was having some sort of episode. Maybe I shouldn't even be driving the car I'd rented at the airport.

She pressed the button to hold the doors open since I hadn't made a move forward. My feet were stuck to the tile floor as if I had glue on the bottom of my tennis shoes.

"Hi."

My hallucination could speak.

"Hi," I said, still not moving. "Are you real?"

Her smile made my heart beat faster. "Yes, I'm real. George told me where you were. I just flew in or I would have been here sooner."

I didn't know if it was her voice or the fact that I was beginning to comprehend that she was actually standing in that elevator, but I finally stepped in and the doors slid shut. There was no one else in the car with us and there was so much I wanted to say, but I didn't even know where to begin. Luckily, I didn't have to say anything. Ashlyn spoke first.

After she reached out and pressed the red emergency stop button bringing the elevator to a shaky halt.

"I want to apologize."

I wanted to sweep her up into my arms. I didn't care what she had to say. She was here.

"You stopped the elevator."

"I did. We need to talk, Kyle."

"This is a hospital, Ash. They need the elevators. You can't stop them."

As much as I wanted to be a spontaneous dude I couldn't help but think this might not be the greatest idea in the world. But it was the cutest and the most romantic. She'd definitely earned points for that. Maybe we'd tell our kids about this someday.

"I'm not mad anymore, Ash. I love you."

"I love you, too. And I'm just so sorry. I read Shelby's book on the plane ride here and it said that couples need to work at their relationships. That agreeing on everything is no guarantee that it will all work out. I'm ready to do the work." She took a deep breath and placed her palms on my chest. I could feel the heat of her skin through the cotton of my button-down shirt. "I sent Gran back to Washington. The rally is cancelled."

She had no idea. George had sent her here and she'd come, but she didn't know.

As for Shelby's book? I had no clue what she was talking about. I'd ask her later.

"It would have been anyway. The engineering report came back, babe. We can save two of the houses and that's what we're going to do."

Her eyes went wide and then she flung herself into my arms. I captured her lips with mine and it was the sweetest kiss I'd ever had with a woman. It said more than we ever could with words.

Reaching over, I pressed the red emergency button and the elevator shuddered for a moment and then began descending. We were still kissing when the doors slid open. A group of people had gathered while waiting and there were a few giggles and one person whistled as we strolled out. Ashlyn's cheeks were pink and mine might have been, too. I wasn't big on public displays but today I'd make an exception.

Leading her to where I'd parked my rental, I loaded her single bag into the trunk and then slid behind the wheel. I still couldn't believe that she was here sitting next to me. It was surreal and wonderful all at the same time.

"I would have been home in a few days."

Smiling, she placed her hand on my mine. A simple gesture but it meant so much. We might not get much sleep back at the hotel. My mind was wandering into other more sensual places. From the look on her face, she was thinking it, too.

"I know, but George suggested I come and I really didn't want to wait." She leaned over and pressed her lips to mine. "Because you're my person, and we're supposed to be together."

Ashlyn and I were surely going to disagree about things in the coming years. We didn't always see eye to eye. But today she'd spoken the truth.

We were supposed to be together.

I hope you enjoyed Kyle and Ashlyn's story! There will be more in the Man Trap series coming soon.
Thank you for reading Tease Him.
Don't miss a thing! Sign up to be notified of Olivia's new releases:
Mailing List
oliviajaymesoptin.instapage.com

About The Author

Olivia Jaymes is a wife, mother, lover of sexy romance, and caffeine addict. She lives with her husband and son in central Florida and spends her days with handsome alpha males and spunky heroines.

She is currently working on a new contemporary romance series – *Man Trap* in addition to her other ongoing series.

Visit Olivia Jaymes at
www.OliviaJaymes.com

Other Titles by Olivia Jaymes

Danger Incorporated

Damsel In Danger

Hiding From Danger

Discarded Heart Novella

Indecent Danger

Embracing Danger

Danger In The Night

Reunited With Danger

Window to Danger

Road to Danger

Unwanted Danger

Cowboy Justice Association

Cowboy Command

Justice Healed

Cowboy Truth

Cowboy Famous

Cowboy Cool

Imperfect Justice

The Deputies

Justice Inked

Justice Reborn

Vengeful Justice

Justice Divided

Seeking Justice

Military Moguls
Champagne and Bullets
Diamonds and Revolvers
Caviar and Covert Ops
Emeralds, Rubies, and Camouflage

Midnight Blue Beach
Wicked After Midnight
Midnight Of No Return
Kiss Midnight Goodbye

The Hollywood Showmance Chronicles
A Kiss For the Cameras
Swinging From A Star
Wild on the Red Carpet
Love in the Spotlight
And the Winner is

www.ingramcontent.com/pod-product-compliance
Lightning Source LLC
Chambersburg PA
CBHW020819260626
47169CB00003B/735

* 9 7 8 1 9 4 4 4 9 0 4 5 4 *